In the Grip of the Druids

Beth Coombe Harris

In the Grip of the Druids

Beth Coombe Harris

MAYFLOWER CHRISTIAN BOOKS
The Publishing Branch of
MAYFLOWER CHRISTIAN BOOKSHOP'S CHARITABLE TRUST
114 Spring Road, Sholing, Southampton, Hants. SO19 2QB

ISBN 0907 821 073

Cover design and line drawings by Ruth Goodridge
Printed and bound in Great Britain by
Itchen Printers Limited,
Southampton

FOREWORD

As a boy I was presented with a copy of this book for regular attendance at Sunday School. I began to read it and could not put it down until I had finished it. Subsequently I read it again - several times.

As a story it gripped me. Its basic framework of historical facts giving insight into the conflict between Christianity and savage paganism in the first two centuries A.D., I later discovered to be well-founded. Miss Harris had researched her background material with careful and discerning patience. There is substantial evidence to support the view that the faith of Christ and His Apostles was firmly established in Britain by the end of the first century A.D; and the British Druids hated and opposed not only the progress of the Roman legions but also the spread of Christianity.

In the wise providence of God, the Roman occupation of Britain was of infinite value to these islands not only culturally and politically, but also spiritually. The story which Miss Harris has woven into this background has in its sequel lessons of devotion and self-denial which each rising generation of young Christians needs to absorb for themselves if they are to be useful in the Lord's service. I found these lessons personally challenging. In these days of materialism and self-centred ambition may they be learned afresh to the glory of God and the extension of His Kingdom.

C.P. Lewis. B.A.

CONTENTS

PUBLISHERS' PREFACE

When Beth Coombe Harris wrote "In the Grip of the Druids" over 50 years ago, there was not the same great interest in the Druids that exists today. Currently, there is a growing fascination with the ideas and behaviour of our pre-Christian Celtic ancestors, especially in view of 'New Age' thinking.

The practice of human sacrifice is an integral part of our story. And it is possible that this issue may be challenged. However, the publishers are satisfied that material available justifies this aspect of the story.

We are particularly grateful to the late Stephen Jack, M.A., of Catshill, near Bromsgrove, for his thorough investigation of the religion and practice of the Druids. He was able to establish clearly the validity of the views and practices of the Druids as set forth by Beth Coombe Harris.

Having read the relevant authorities, and having made contact with the British Museum, Stephen Jack has furnished the publishers with all the material they needed to vindicate this aspect of the story. "The Lindow man - the Body in the Bog", published by the British Museum in 1986, by Stead, Bourke and Brothwell, is particularly helpful. Dr. I.M. Stead is Deputy Keeper of the Department of Prehistoric and Romano/British Antiquities, British Museum; Don Brothwell is Reader in Zoo Archaeology at the Institute of Archaeology, London; and J.B. Bourke is in the Department of Surgery, University Hospital, Nottingham. The famous 'bog-man' was not mugged but the subject of a ritual killing. Stephen Jack also referred to other authorities at length, to the complete satisfaction of the publishers.

Beth Coombe Harris' accuracy in the matter of human sacrifice, as well as background detail, is particularly well seen in her description of the horrific "wicker man" in Chapter 24. Here, she describes the cage shaped like a human figure in which prisoners were sacrificed by being burnt alive. This appalling practice is well documented.

Some may object to the presentation of history by means of a fictitious story line. This is not without precedent, and can be used to bring home the reality of events long-forgotten. Others may object to the use of fiction to convey Christian truth. We need to remember the example of Scripture where fiction is used by means of parables. Bunyan's "Pilgrim's Progress" is seldom criticised because it was an allegory. The description of Hopeful's conversion in his discussion with Christian is purely fictitious but it is so Biblical in the concept of the whole experience that it comes across with reality and force. Some Christian fiction is so 'romantic' that it raises justifiable objections, but Beth Coombe Harris takes her story through human and Christian experience in such a way that it is credible.

It is a sad fact that there is so little 'easy' reading that is not superficial in a spiritual sense. We should not always have to choose 'heavy' reading in order to be edified. Great efforts are made by the media to entertain us, and so it is easy for the Christian to neglect weighty matters because they are couched in heavy forms. It is good to have a text that is both easy to read *and* profitable. We are grateful to Paul Lewis, Pastor of Welcome Hall Evangelical Church, Catshill, for his Foreword.He introduced the book to us, with a view to publication. We are grateful to Ruth Goodridge for the excellent illustrations that add greatly to the presentation of the book.

In this historical novel Beth Coombe Harris uses her careful research and knowledge of Christian experience to bring to life the undoubted triumph of the Gospel over paganism nearly 2,000 years ago. A book like this can be an encouragement to us in these days when Pagan darkness is reasserting itself. We pray that this may be so.

The Publishers.

CHARACTERS

Venissa - a young maiden
Hulda - her mother
Cynvelin - her father
Amelia - the family servant
Elfrida - Venissa's aunt
Osmond - Elfrida's son
Alaric - a family friend
Griselda - an old lady visited by the family
Leirwg - Chief Druid
Bernard - a travelling evangelist and storyteller
Julia - a young child captured by the Druids
Felicius - a Roman Soldier
Placidia - his wife
Marcus, Canace, & Flora - his children

Chapter 1

In The Year Of Our Lord, 150.

ALARIC, tall and strongly built for his fifteen years, strode along the forest path. He whistled as he advanced, carrying a fairly big coracle on his back with ease, while in one hand he held fishing tackle. He intended having a morning on the river; combining pleasure with work, he expected to be rewarded with a good catch of fish and so justify to his father the few hours spent away from his usual tasks. Not that his parent was difficult to please. Alaric being the only child and his father an elderly man, the lad was indulged more than most boys in those days.

He paused on his way to examine a plant. Was it the sacred vervain? If so, he must report the find to Leirwg, the head of the

Druidical priests in his neighbourhood. As he stooped over the plant, he heard voices behind him and turned to see who was coming.

His eye brightened and he exclaimed: "Ah! here come Venissa and her attendant, Amelia. Where can they be going? I'll wait for them".

The young people greeted each other with pleasure, and, in reply to Alaric's inquiry, Venissa explained: "We are going to see my old nurse, Griselda. My mother wished to send her some eggs".

"It is a long walk to Griselda's hut, let me take you by the river", Alaric said eagerly.

Venissa hesitated at first but yielded after a moment or two to Alaric's suggestion. She turned to her attendant and put out her hand for the basket the woman was carrying, saying, "Amelia, you can remain here until I return".

"But, Mistress Venissa", responded Amelia, "your mother said I was not to let you out of my sight. I shall be in trouble if anything happens to you."

Alaric laughed happily: "What harm could reach her if she is with me, Amelia? You need have no fear".

The slave woman, in spite of her protest, seemed willing to be persuaded to remain behind and, when Venissa added: "You can follow us along the river path; we shall scarcely be out of your sight," she handed over the basket, and the girl and boy ran lightly down to the river, where Alaric quickly launched the coracle; both sprang in, and Alaric paddled off. The coracle, made of wicker-work and covered with skin, was a safe craft, easy to propel.

"Poor old Amelia," Venissa said, as she watched the woman trying to keep pace with them.

The boat shot ahead and Amelia gave up the chase. She could only wait until her young charge returned. She sat down on a mossy bank and gave herself up to thought. Sad thoughts they were. Some twenty years before, she had been a happy, young wife and mother in a northern part of Britain, when a party of raiders, seeking both slaves and pearls, the latter to be obtained from the river mussels in the Dee, swooped down on the woman and carried her off with some others, far, far from her home, to the southern part of the land. She had been put up for sale in Caer Isca (Exeter) and purchased by Cynvelin, Venissa's father. Cynvelin, and his wife, Hulda, were kind to their slaves in comparison with many masters and mistresses in those days, but Amelia never forgot the home and friends from which she had been stolen.

Meanwhile, sounds of laughter came from the boat as Alaric and Venissa enjoyed one another's company.

Presently, Alaric ran the coracle into a little creek of white stones, where willows and alders overhung in a fringe-like veil of green, and the two proceeded to climb a steep, rugged path between rock boulders and massive trees, finally emerging, hot and panting, on a small clearing where a solitary hut stood.

"What a safe place to hide in if one were in peril," Alaric said as he looked around.

"There is no safe hiding place from our priests," Venissa answered and her face shadowed as she mentioned the word.

It was indeed a lonely spot. A small wattle-hut stood in the centre of the clearing; the branches of an oak tree blasted by lightning stretched over the low roof, looking like some grim and awful guardian. In the doorway of the hut an old woman sat, toothless and wrinkled, and by her side was a huge black cat. A small fire of twigs smouldered on the ground nearby, over which hung a pot containing some boiling liquid.

Their errand quickly done, Venissa and Alaric said good-bye to Griselda, and ran down the path to the river.

"Let us rest awhile here," Alaric said, seating himself on the white strand. "It is so cool and pleasant. The water lapping on the stones makes me feel lazy."

Venissa flung herself down willingly and Alaric watched her. Her long fair hair reached far below her waist; it was kept back from her forehead by a thin coronet of gold, and she wore gold bangles on her arms and ankles. Her dress of loosely-woven, thin, woollen material was dyed a golden brown shade and caught at the waist by a girdle of enamel-work.[1] Her eyes were blue, varying in shade according to her moods; just now they looked dark and almost gloomy.

The two were silent for a time, then Alaric said, "Venissa, I never knew why old Griselda left your parents' home and went to live in the woods. I was away on a pilgrimage with my father when that happened".

"Oh! don't you know? The other servants got the idea that she was a witch, and truly she looks like one. My father and mother were afraid they would do her harm; indeed, they did start to stone her, but father rescued her. She is quite safe where she is, not one of our slaves would dare venture near her; they say the clearing is haunted, an evil spirit dwells in the blasted oak, how otherwise could a sacred tree be struck? And, indeed, it is hollow. Did you notice how readily Amelia agreed to stay behind? I knew she was terribly frightened when my mother gave her the order to accompany me but she dare not protest."

"You are not afraid, Venissa?"

"No, certainly not. My father has always taught me to be brave, and I know old Griselda would not harm a hair of my head; no, I don't fear her."

"What do you fear, Venissa? I think you became sad at times to-day. Is anything troubling you? What are you thinking about?"

"I am thinking of my cousin, Osmond. You know the priests have sent him to the River Dee to bring back sacred water".

"Well, that need not trouble you, Venissa. He will be back again in time. Is it that you miss him? But I don't see how that can be, for, now that he is in training at the University at Caer Isca to become a Druidical priest, you seldom see him".

"No, it is not that I miss him. I know he will be back in a few months. He has promised to bring me pearls from the sacred river. [2]

---

[1] "In the art of enamel British workmen stood unrivalled."

[2] 'The pearl fisheries of Britain existed before the Roman invasion, and the hope of acquiring pearls was an inducement to Caesar to attempt the conquest of the country. A breastplate studded with British pearls was dedicated to Venus and suspended in her temple in Rome by Caesar. They were not obtained from oysters but a peculiar species of mussel.

But don't you know what that is a sign of, the fetching of sacred water?"

"I suppose you mean the priests intend having a sacrifice. You need not let that worry you, Venissa".

"It does worry me, Alaric. Suppose I should be needed as an offering?"

Alaric sprang to his feet. "You, Venissa! Impossible. You, the only child of your parents, the apple of your father's eye, the darling of your mother's heart. Does she not always call you 'tatta' (darling)?"

"That is just it, Alaric. Leirwg says the more precious the possession, the more acceptable is the offering to the gods. I fear he has his eye on me".

Alaric's face grew crimson with indignation.

"Venissa, I would give my life to save you, but what can I do?"

"Nothing", she replied gloomily.

"Why are the priests contemplating a special sacrifice just now, do you know?" Alaric asked.

"Because of the drought," replied Venissa. "Leirwg says the gods must be angry and they must be appeased. You see there has been no sacrifice for some years, other than the regular ones three times a year, then it has only been a bull. Now, if human beings are to be offered, it will have to be done in secret, for the Romans will not allow it if they know of it; they have suppressed it in other places, but here in Dynvaint (Devonshire) we are far from their camps".

"Yes, I know all that. The Romans want to break the power of the Druids, and a good thing too. I hate them. I hate the gods. I hate religion".

"Oh hush, hush, Alaric! If we should be overheard! Remember poor Cerman; what a terrible fate was his".

"Yes, I do remember and it only makes me hate them all the more. Why should they have the power to excommunicate a man? Do you remember, Venissa, how they struck his name out of the roll of the parchment of our tribe? How they branded his forehead? How they

---

"And Britain's ancient shores great pearls produce."—Marbodwus.

pierced his breast, and poured the blood drawn from it on his head, saying ‘The blood of the man thus accursed be on his own head’? Then everybody was forbidden to speak to him or give him food, and now probably his skeleton lies unburied in some dense part of the forest”.

Venissa shuddered.

“Alaric, I never understood why Cerman was excommunicated. He seemed so good and kind”.

“I don’t know either. I was only twelve when that happened, and we are forbidden to mention his name in our family, but I did hear a whisper that he had renounced the worship of our gods, and worshipped some strange new god. Oh, how I hate religion!” Alaric said once again. “But there, let us forget all this and be happy, Venissa”.

“Forget the priests and the sacrifice! I do try to forget, and sometimes I succeed, but old Griselda brought it to my mind today. She muttered, ‘a fair offering, a fair offering indeed!’ ”

“Detestable old woman”, Alaric interrupted.

“It brought it all back to mind, Alaric. That last sacrifice when we were tiny. My poor cousin Ida, Osmond’s sister. Poor Ida; I can see it all now. The big wicker cage filled with human beings. The fire, the crowds! There were not enough prisoners-of-war to satisfy the gods, so the priests said, and Ida and some others were given”.

“Yes, I know. I never could understand your uncle and aunt. First giving Ida for sacrifice, and now your aunt has allowed Osmond to leave her to be trained as a priest”.

“Aunt is deeply religious, Alaric. Besides, you remember at the time of the sacrifice, uncle was very ill, and Leirwg told aunt that the gods would be pleased and restore him to health, if the child was given, but it was no good — uncle died just the same. Now, I believe aunt thinks it a great honour to be the mother of a priest; it is always reckoned so. Osmond will never have to fight, never pay taxes, and be reverenced by all. In time he may even become an Arch-priest like Leirwg”.

"I'm not so sure, Venissa. The Romans are changing all that. It is useless for the Druids to meet them with curses - they don't care a bronze anklet for that sort of thing; they retaliate with spears and swords, and the priests will have to yield; they have in many places, and the sooner they come here the better, I say. When I went on that pilgrimage with father, we learnt that the Romans realise they will never have a peaceful occupation while the Druids stir up the people to rebellion, so the orders have come from Rome that the Druids are to be suppressed, their groves cut down, the sacrifices forbidden. In the north and east of our land, the Romans have partly accomplished this, but here in the far west the old religion lingers. We are still in the grip of the Druids. I only wish we could be delivered from them and all religion done away with".

"But, Alaric, will not the gods be terribly angry if we cease to worship them and make sacrifices to them?"

"I don't believe it would make any difference", said the lad stoutly.

Venissa sighed, and Alaric, seeing how troubled she looked, tried to turn her thoughts into another channel.

"Venissa, I must get some fish or I shall get into trouble. I promised to bring some home with me".

Both sprang up and set to work. They were experts at the job, and soon had a few fish, enough, Alaric considered, to show for his morning on the river; so the young people hastened to return, realising it was nearly noon and they would be expected in their respective homes.

Chapter 2.

The Little Captive.

THE summer weeks passed uneventfully; the drought continued; day after day, the sun shone in a cloudless sky; the brooks dwindled to a mere thread or disappeared entirely; the springs grew low and some failed; the women had added to their daily tasks the burden of fetching water, sometimes from a long distance, wherever there was a living, bubbling spring.

The Druids thundered forth to the anxious people fiery denouncements. The gods were angry and must be appeased. Gifts were showered at the feet of the priests. Gifts in kind — cattle, grain, gold, pearls; bronze coins also were brought, but the priests hinted that a nobler sacrifice was required; many a fair maiden and stalwart youth shivered with apprehension, while the parents' hearts were heavy with fear. They knew only too well the power of the priests and the terror of the gods. Fathers and mothers might wish to save their children, but such was the awe instilled in their hearts by the leaders of their false worship that, should a priest name a certain person, child, grown-up, bond or free, as desired by the gods, it was impossible to withhold that one. It would be useless to attempt it, for public opinion was, as now, strong, and the people would insist that calamities would fall on all if the sacrifice was not made.[3]

One fair day, early in September, Osmond returned from his journey to the River Dee. He brought with him flagons of the sacred water, without which the priests would not carry out the complicated ritual of the sacrifices. He brought also the gift of pearls he had promised his cousin, Venissa, and hastened to present them to her, as soon as he had reported himself to his chief, Leirwg, and greeted his mother. Osmond was in a cheerful mood, for Leirwg had pronounced his satisfaction at the way the young man had performed his task. He had granted him leave of absence from his college in Caer Isca for a month, graciously telling him to take a holiday, save that he might be called upon to perform some service in connection with the proposed religious festival and sacrifice which the Druids had decided must take place at the autumn worship of the gods. The Druids held three special festivals each year; on May the first; one in the autumn; one in mid-winter, when the sacred mistletoe was gathered by the priests.

Venissa expressed pleasure at the gift of the pearls, but her face grew grave when Osmond said he had successfully brought the sacred water.

"Oh, Osmond, I wish you had spilt it on the journey".

---

[3] 'Hume, the historian, writes: "No idolatrous worship ever obtained such an ascendancy over mankind as that of the Ancient Britons. The spoils of war were often devoted to their divinities by the Druids; they punished with horrible tortures all those who dared to secrete any portion of the consecrated offering. These treasures, kept in woods and forests, were secured by no other guard than the terrors of religion."

"Why, Venissa, the gods would have been angry with me had I been so careless. You would not wish me to incur the wrath of the gods, to say nothing of the displeasure of Leirwg".

Alaric, who was present, laughed sardonically.

"Leirwg's wrath would vent itself in a more active fashion than that of the gods, I reckon".

"Whatever do you mean, Alaric?" Osmond asked. "Man's power is limited, but the gods—" Osmond broke off and shivered.

"I'm not so sure. I doubt if these old gods have any power. It is the priests that have the power, and well they know it".

"Peace, Alaric, say no more. If I did my duty I should report you to Leirwg, and you would have to take the consequence. I should be sorry to get you into trouble, so please stop making such wild remarks in my presence", Osmond spoke gravely.

"Ah, well, maybe silence is wisdom", Alaric answered lightly.

Osmond turned to Venissa who was fingering her pearls.

"Tell me, Venissa, why you wished the sacred water had been spilt?"

"Osmond, don't you understand? Without the sacred water the sacrifice could not be made at the autumn festival. Who are to be the victims? The priests have not yet said".

Osmond grew pale.

"Venissa! Venissa! Surely you are not in danger. You who are the 'tatta' of your parents. Leirwg will certainly remember how, before you were born, six little babies were born to your parents and died in infancy and then, when the seventh came, a bonny boy, your parents, Cynvelin and Hulda, sacrificed him to appease the wrath of the gods, and how the gods accepted their offering and showed their pleasure by giving you to them and keeping you in health all your life".

"But, do you not remember that the priests say, 'the greater the treasure, the more acceptable it is to the gods'? And now they tell us that if an offering is not made and rain does not fall, many people will die of thirst, and sickness will break out among us".

"Do not be troubled, dear Venissa, before the time of the autumn festival, rain may fall, or, what is very likely, our men will return with prisoners of war. I heard on my travels that there is fighting going on in the region of Glevum (Gloucester). Then the priests will be satisfied to offer the prisoners, and our own youths and maidens will be safe".

So saying, Osmond departed and Alaric and Venissa were left.

"Alaric", said Venissa, as soon as her cousin was out of hearing, "why do you sneer at the gods? I fear for you. I pray you do not anger them".

"Look here, Venissa, I am inclined to put them to the test. If I speak against them, ignore their worship, neglect them, let us wait and see if anything terrible happens to me; if not, we shall know there is nothing in what the priests say".

"Don't, Alaric. If Leirwg hears that you have said this, he will punish you severely".

"That's just the point. It is the priests we need to fear, not the gods. The priests threaten us with the wrath of the gods, but that is all a farce; the priests mean us to fear them".

A few days later, Alaric sought Venissa. Great excitement showed itself in his every action.

"Venissa", he exclaimed, "Osmond has sent me to tell you, prisoners-of-war are brought in. They will be here shortly. I am going along the road to watch. Ask your mother if you may accompany me".

Venissa sought her mother's permission. She found that her father, Cynvelin, as chief of his village, had already heard the news, and gone forth to issue orders as to the destiny of the prisoners.

Venissa's mother gave her permission, bidding an attendant to accompany her daughter. It was a long wait before the tramp of feet proclaimed the drawing near of the men of war and their captives.

It was a sorry sight, at least, so Venissa thought, although many of the onlookers and the men of war seemed triumphant. They passed along the narrow, rutty track which was the only road leading to the village of Cynvelin. Men, women, boys and girls had been captured, some twenty in all, each guarded by a stalwart man.

Venissa regarded them, more or less, indifferently, until, at the end of the procession, one of the victorious party walked alone, carrying in his arms a beautiful child. She was too young to keep pace with the others and seemed content in the man's arms. There were traces of tears on the little one's face, but evidently her captor had succeeded in quieting her and, unconscious of her peril, poor child, she looked round with interest.

"Look, Alaric, look!", Venissa whispered to her companion. "Is she not beautiful"?

Indeed, the child was exceptionally pretty. Big, brown, velvety eyes; thick, dark hair curling round her head; olive skin, yet clear and flushed with a healthy colour, she was dressed in a richly-embroidered garment, and on her arm was a gold bangle curiously engraved. Venissa had not time at that moment to observe all these details, she only realised a charming child had been taken captive.

"Alaric, who can she be?" she asked.

"Not one of our nationality", Alaric replied. "I believe she is a Roman".

"What a shame to take a little thing like that! She can't be more than three years old".

It was Alaric's turn to advise caution. He was reckless for himself, but not where Venissa was concerned.

"Hush, be careful what you say", he whispered.

The two followed the procession until the village green was reached and, from a little distance, they watched the Druids inspecting the prisoners. Cynvelin was speaking; it seemed he did not altogether approve of the captives being given over to the Druids, but Leirwg and the other priests urged the claims of the gods and spoke with authority. Leirwg considered himself of greater importance than even the chief of the tribe; in the name of religion he expected obedience from Cynvelin. And, gripped by the long habit of submission, Cynvelin yielded.

It was apparent that the capture of the child gave special pleasure. Venissa and Alaric caught snatches of conversation.

"A fit offering for the gods".

"A patrician child evidently".

"How was she taken?"

Neither Venissa or Alaric could hear quite distinctly the reply of the man who held the child in his arms.

Venissa just heard the words, “Strayed away from her nurse”.

At the word “nurse”, the little one burst into tears, sobbing piteously, calling “nurse, nurse”.

Alaric was about to spring forward, but Venissa restrained him.

“Don’t do anything now, Alaric. Let us talk it over and see if we can think of a plan to save her. I want to go home, I cannot bear seeing these poor things”.

So they turned away, discussing as they went as to what they could do, but they could think of nothing feasible.

Venissa’s last remark was, “I wonder if Osmond could suggest something. Perhaps he could persuade Leirwg to sell the child to father. You know, Alaric, Leirwg is much attached to Osmond”.

Alaric shook his head gloomily.

“Try if you like, Venissa. But I fear Leirwg’s heart is too hard to be moved by anybody”.

At the first opportunity, Venissa approached her cousin on the matter. Osmond was sincerely fond of the girl and hated to see the tears gather in her eyes, but he said he dare not interfere. Leirwg and the other priests considered the child the cream of the offering which they planned to make, as soon as the right day came for the autumn festival. No rain had fallen, and something must be done to save themselves and the people from the suffering caused by the drought.

Chapter 3.

A Forlorn Hope.

ALARIC and Osmond were both very keen to save the little victim for Venissa's sake, and at last Osmond thought of a possible plan. He made his way over to Venissa's hut and when he was sure that no one could overhear their conversation he told her all about his idea.

The prisoners were all kept in an enclosure, a square of land surrounded by a rough mortarless wall made of huge stones. The wall was low and easy to scale for, as all the captives were heavily weighted with chains, there was no possibility of escape and little guardianship was needed. One Druidical priest patrolled night and day and, on the morning of the day that he sought Venissa, Osmond had just been told that he was to be on duty that night.

“Venissa”, he said, after greeting his cousin, “I think I can help you. I am on guard tonight. If you and Alaric like to make a raid, now is your chance. I will see that the child is sleeping at the south end of the enclosure. You take your chance when I am on the north side”.

“Oh-h, Osmond! But what will Leirwg say?”

“I think I can tell a tale that will satisfy him. I shall say a huge wolf sprang over the wall and, although I rushed to the defence, it had seized the child by her garment and carried her off before I could intervene”.

Venissa could not help laughing.

“But can you hide her anywhere if you get her away?” Osmond asked.

Venissa thought a minute. Then she clapped her hands gleefully.

“Why, yes; Alaric and I can take her to my old nurse, Griselda. No one goes near her, you know, because of the blasted oak; besides, so many think she is a witch. Do find Alaric and send him to me”.

“I don’t want to be seen talking to Alaric. Send a messenger and ask him to come to you”.

This was easily done, and Alaric soon appeared. Together the two took counsel. Alaric at first objected strongly to Venissa taking any part in the scheme. She could direct, he would carry her ideas out faithfully, but he objected to Venissa running any risks - and there were many. The risk of detection, of wild beasts and, perhaps even still more to be dreaded than boars or wolves, wild men.

But Venissa was by no means lacking in courage. She argued that the little maiden would be less likely to be alarmed if she were present, for more than once since the child had been brought to the village, Venissa had obtained permission to feed her with dainties. So Alaric gave way as, in fact, he always did when Venissa coaxed him. Alaric inquired if Venissa would tell her father and mother of their scheme. Venissa was emphatic in her reply.

“No; certainly not. Don’t you see, Alaric, the fewer people who know about this, the less likely it is to become known? Besides, one never knows how one’s parents will look at things. Mother is so afraid of the wrath of the gods and in awe of Leirwg, and father hates anything like rebellion or law-breaking; they may forbid my interfering. If they know nothing, they cannot forbid it. If, after the sacrifice, I have to tell them, in order to get their aid in providing for little Julia, then I can say, if they take exception to my action, 'Of course, I did not know you would object' ".

Alaric laughed.

"Artful girl. How did you learn to manage your parents like this?"

Venissa tossed her head, pretending to be annoyed at being called 'artful'. However, they both quickly grew grave for they realised they were undertaking no easy task. First of all, they had to get away from their homes unobserved; then the child had to be removed noiselessly and, finally, there was the long walk through the forest and the steep climb to the hut.

"I will leave home directly it is dark", Alaric said, "and come here. When you hear three owl hoots in succession, creep out and we will go forward".

Venissa agreed, and Alaric continued, "Did you say the child is called Julia and does she speak our language?"

"Yes, she calls herself 'Juli' and speaks a few words that I can understand, but it is not much; I am not sure whether it is baby prattle or a foreign tongue".

Alaric went off, and Venissa sat thinking of what she had undertaken to do; in spite of the risk they were running she felt excited, for she loved an adventure. The thing she really dreaded was discovery by the priests, when terrible punishment would fall upon the offenders. However, loved as she was by her parents, Venissa had not been pampered; she had been trained to accomplish difficult tasks; to share in the hunt; to catch and ride a high-spirited horse, and Venissa's ambition, as it was of every other British girl, was to be as brave as the great Queen Boadicea, of whom the bards sang.

It was the bards who, wandering up and down the country, kept the knowledge of history in the minds of the people, as they sang their songs telling of noble deeds. Every British girl had heard of Queen Boadicea, tall and majestic with a voice as deep as a man's; her hair, in long golden tresses, coming to her hips, and over her tartan dress wearing a military cloak. The bards sang of her addressing the Britons before leading them to battle, in tones of passionate appeal, and how, although at first successful, after a terrible combat, the Romans conquered, and poor, brave, pitiful Boadicea took poison.

When darkness fell, Venissa lay apparently asleep on her couch, keeping the bear-skin rug well over her shoulders so that if, by chance, her mother came into her room, she would not discover that her daughter had not undressed; but in reality, the girl was never more alert, while the noises in the household gradually died down and all was still. Venissa had not long to wait; a soft but clear "tu-whit, tu-whoo" sounded forth three times in succession. Venissa rose silently, and on her bare feet glided noiselessly from her room without hindrance, and succeeded in joining Alaric.

"I hope the child won't cry out", Alaric whispered as they proceeded to the spot where the prisoners were kept.

"I don't think she will, she knows me. Several times I have been allowed to visit her and give her sweetmeats. I've brought some with me now, and this wolf skin rug to wrap her in", Venissa answered.

Stealthily the two drew near the desired spot and watched. It was a night of half lights, for the moon was nearly full but heavy clouds now and again obscured her shining.

Presently, Alaric and Venissa saw Osmond on his slow march. He passed close by them but gave no sign of having seen them, but he apparently had done so, for he lingered long on reaching the north side of the enclosure, thus affording Venissa ample time to climb the low wall and reach the little sleeper's side. Venissa stooped over the child; whispering kindly words, she gently raised her. Julia opened her eyes and Venissa popped a sweetmeat into her mouth, thus quieting any fear that might have caused the child to cry. Seeing who her visitor was, Julia nestled sleepily in Venissa's arms, and made no demur at being handed over to Alaric. Delighted at their success so far, the two hurried off on their long walk, and at last reached Griselda's hut without untoward incident.

The old woman was easily roused, but it was some time before she took in what was required of her. She was not at all willing to undertake the custody of little Julia, and Venissa had to be almost imperious in her orders. At last Griselda, accustomed all her life to yield obedience to her owners, gave in, and Julia was handed over to the old woman's care.

Poor Julia broke into a wail when she saw Venissa was preparing to leave her. Venissa would have lingered, if Alaric had not been emphatic in hastening her away.

"Venissa, we must go; day will dawn before we get back and all will be discovered if we do not hurry!"

So Venissa, promising Griselda and Julia that she would come again quite soon and bring food, tore herself away from the crying child.

"Poor little thing, I do hope Griselda will be kind to her", Venissa said, as together they scrambled down the rough track which led to the river path. Alaric made no reply. He was too busy assisting Venissa and hastening her footsteps for conversation. Hurry they must, if they were to get back before day, so they rushed along as fast as broken rocks, overhanging bushes and holes of many kinds would permit. At last, they stood outside Venissa's home and she whispered: "Praise be to the gods that we have succeeded so well".

Venissa might not have been so fervent in praise of the gods had she been able to overhear Griselda's whispered remarks when left alone.

"Now, what am I to do?" muttered the old woman, who always talked to herself in a half-audible whisper. "Brave the wrath of my little mistress and deliver the child back to the priests, or brave the wrath of the gods and keep the child".

The wrath of the mistress might result in a shortage of creature comforts, but the wrath of the gods--who could say what that might mean?

At that moment, a flash of summer lightning flitted across the sky, and old Griselda, terrified of lightning, flung herself on the ground grovelling in her fears.

"Ah, the gods have begun to show their anger already, that settles it".

Chapter 4.

Saved At The Last Moment.

NEXT morning, Venissa slept late. Her mother came and looked at her daughter and marvelled at her slumbers. However, she gave orders that Venissa was not to be disturbed, so it came to pass that it was noon before the girl awoke, and was surprised on springing from her couch and pulling back the little wooden shutter that barred the window of her room, to find the sun was high in the sky.

It was a busy scene that met her eye as she emerged from her sleeping apartment, but one to which she had been accustomed all her life. Within the stockade, which was of some considerable height, broken by four entrances, were a number of wattle huts, that is, made of wicker-work and daubed with clay. In the centre of the enclosure was a large roofed-in space, the roof being supported by stout poles; it was open on all sides and was used when all the members of the household and farm workers were gathered together. No hut was sufficiently large to accommodate them, for Cynvelin, as the chief of his tribe and a wealthy man, owned an immense number of slaves.

Both inside the stockade and outside, these slaves were busy, some cutting wood with stone axes, marvellously sharpened; some preparing the mid-day meal, cooking it on an open fire; others were spinning, others weaving, using chalk weights to stretch the warp and long combs to push the woof into position; again, another set of workers were busy at moulding cups and various vessels from clay, this pottery being simply but prettily decorated with various patterns, dots, circles, crosses, and so on.

Around the homestead were cultivated plots of land, where flax and wheat were grown.

Among all the workers Venissa's mother moved, encouraging or admonishing as it seemed good to her. She greeted her daughter with a gentle smile.

"You slept late, my child", she said.

"Yes, Mother. I was tired", Venissa replied without a trace of self-consciousness.

"Well, you are in time to call your father to the meal. I see the salmon is well-cooked and there is a dish of beaver and dumplings which your father likes well; Amelia has a fresh brewing of mead and you can bring the curds and whey and the bread". After the mid-day meal, Cynvelin invited his daughter to accompany him on an expedition.

"Venissa", he said, "I have to visit Leirwg. He told me yesterday that today he would have fixed the date of the autumn festival; there are many arrangements to make as it is to be a great ceremony. The gods must be appeased and the sooner the better, I consider, for this drought is becoming a serious matter. However, what I was going to suggest, is that you might like to go with me and visit the little captive girl".

"Thank you, father", Venissa answered demurely, but her eyes twinkled as she thought of her last night's escapade and of the vacant place there would be in the prisoners' enclosure.

But it needed all Venissa's presence of mind and self-control not to exclaim in dismay when she arrived on the spot, for there on the ground and chained to a stout post, lay little Julia, her face tear-stained, her eyes big with fright.

Leirwg came to meet them and, looking at Venissa with his piercing eyes, said: "There is a strange story about the child".

"What is that?" Cynvelin asked.

"Last night, your nephew, Osmond, was on guard and he says that a big wolf jumped the wall and seized the child ; the creature was gone before Osmond could intervene. This morning, old Griselda brought the child here, saying she had found her wandering at dawn near her hut. But, mark you, I have found no trace of the wolf's teeth on her body or clothing, although I have searched carefully. She must be kept safe from wolves, or any other intruder now; she is chained by day and at night will sleep under guard in the hut".

Venissa's heart sank within her. How she hated Leirwg and the cruel practices of the priests under the name of religion. At the moment, she could do nothing for little Julia except try to comfort her with loving words. Leirwg made no objection to Venissa entering the enclosure, so, sitting on the ground, she took Julia on her lap. The child clung to her friend and, speaking more distinctly than usual, said, "Julia wants her mother".

Venissa determined to make one more effort to save the poor little victim. Was not her father ever indulgent to her? She would appeal to him.

On their way home, Cynvelin paved the way for her confidence by saying: "My daughter, can you tell me why Leirwg looked at you so piercingly when telling the story of the child and the wolf?"

"Do not be displeased with me, father", Venissa said, and then told him all that she and Alaric had done on the previous night. Cynvelin scarcely knew whether to blame or praise, but Venissa turned the scale in her favour by saying: "Father, you have always taught me to be brave and seek to help the unfortunate".

Cynvelin smiled.

"It is your father who is to blame! Is that it? Well, listen; I am proud of your courage, but my commands are that you never again leave the enclosure after dark. It is too dangerous, Venissa. Believe me, my child, you do not understand half the risk you ran. Praise be to the gods, you were kept in safety; it is evident you are under their care. Still, I can quite understand your disappointment that it was all in vain".

"Father", Venissa stood still and faced her parent, lifting her dainty face to meet his gaze, "Father, will you not buy Julia and give her to me for my little slave; my very own, I mean? Leirwg loves gold and land; perhaps, he will be persuaded if you offer a big price. Come back now, dear father, and try".

Cynvelin laughed heartily.

"You bewitch me, Venissa, with your pleading eyes. Well, come back; I can but offer".

Alas, Leirwg was adamant. His eyes were cold and stony. Venissa besought; Cynvelin offered an immense price; the little helpless one looked up from the ground, not really comprehending what was taking place, and yet the pathos of her face was in itself a plea, but all was in vain; Leirwg refused to yield. He seemed to be enjoying his power to oppose Cynvelin and Venissa and said frigidly: "You make an impossible suggestion; she is dedicated to the gods".

Venissa's eyes flashed angrily, her patience was exhausted. She might have poured forth a torrent of words, but her father placed a firm hand on her shoulder, saying: "Peace, Venissa. Leirwg knows what is best. We cannot interpret the wishes of the gods as he can. Has he not had twenty years of training at the university at Caer Isca? Has he not practised the rites of religion for another twenty years or more? Is he not the chosen Arch-Druid? Come, my child, we can do no more".

With eyes blinded with tears, Venissa allowed her father to lead her away.

When out of sight of the priest, Cynvelin placed his arm around his daughter and sought to comfort her, at the same time giving a word of warning.

"My child, you must have a care. You must not anger the priests; if they should call the curse of the gods on us, better by far that you had never been born, for he whom the gods curse can only live in misery".

"Oh, father, Alaric says he thinks the gods are nothing, but he hates the priests and he hates religion, and so, I think, do I".

"Alaric is a rash lad; he does not know what he is saying. I must have a word with him. His old father is too indulgent, I fear, and the boy is allowed too much freedom of thought and action".

The two walked in silence for a time; then, Venissa said suddenly: "Father, I have just thought of something. If the Romans knew we were going to have a religious festival and sacrifice human beings, they would come and stop it. Alaric says they have done so in many places and even burnt the priests in their own fires. Oh, if we could only send to Aqua Salis (Bath) or to Glevum (Gloucester), they have camps there!"

"My child, we must not side with those who would destroy our ancient religion. Who can say whether our priests are right and that the gods demand a sacrifice? If it is so, we dare not interfere. You must forget the child and, when I go to Isca, (Exeter) I will see if I cannot secure you a little slave".

"Thank you, father", Venissa replied, adding to herself: "It won't be Julia, and I do love that poor little mite".

The fateful day drew near for the terrible sacrifice. All was in readiness; the huge wicker cage which was to hold the victims was prepared; the hay to light the fire was at the appointed spot, and there seemed no chance of escape for Julia or the other captives.

Then, two days before the sacrifice was to have been made, rain fell. It began in slow, heavy drops, increasing in volume as the day advanced; the sky was black and a steady, continuous downpour kept up all day, all the night and all the following day.

"The gods have had mercy on us. The gods are no longer angry", was heard from many lips, and then came a rumour, a whisper here and there; one spoke of it to another until all had heard: “The Romans are coming: the sacrifice will be forbidden”.

The priests listened and hesitated. They remembered tidings of terrible happenings in other districts; they had no desire to be caught in the deed and flung on to their own fires. It was announced that, as soon as the rain ceased, the proposed victims would be for sale and a sacred white bull would be offered in lieu of the prisoners.

Cynvelin hastened to purchase Julia. Leirwg made him pay heavily in lands, goods and coin, but Cynvelin did not care, if his gift to his daughter gave her pleasure.

The day of the great festival passed. No Roman appeared.

“It was but a rumour, I believe”, Cynvelin said to Hulda his wife that evening. “I wonder who was responsible for starting it?”

Venissa, who heard the remark, stooped over little Julia to hide a smile. She had had a secret conversation with Alaric that day, and both had rejoiced at the way he had succeeded in his ruse.

Chapter 5.

Felicius And His Family.

THERE was great grief and consternation in a Roman villa in the neighbourhood of Glevum (Gloucester), the home of Felicius and his wife, Placidia. It was a spacious dwelling, built on four sides of a square, around which ran a veranda, from which access was gained to the various rooms. One part of the building, called *the villa urbana,* consisted of the rooms occupied by the family—dining-room, sitting-rooms, bedrooms, bathrooms; another part, *the villa rustica,* was occupied by the slaves; and the third part, *the villa fructuaria,* contained the stores. The lower part of the house was of stone, the upper part, of wood, resembling the half-timbered houses of later date.

The rooms were warmed by hypocausts (flues); the floors of the rooms were raised, a series of pillars were erected under the flooring of tiles, so that there was a space of some feet between the earth and the actual floor of the rooms. On the pillars was laid down a thickness of concrete which formed the foundation for the tessellated floors of the apartments occupied by the Roman and his family. The pattern of the floor was elaborate, composed of cubes of stone of various colours, white, green, yellow, red, black, so arranged in the centre to form a picture. To introduce warmth into this cold flooring, hot air from a furnace was circulated in the flues beneath, the furnace being kept alight by a constant supply of wood.

The room in which Felicius and his wife were seated was beautifully and artistically furnished; solid, well-made couches were draped with costly silks; bronze lamps hung from the ceiling; there were carved tables and chairs and folding stools. Ornaments in Samian pottery stood on shelves, or in niches in the wall; these were a fine red colour with a highly-polished surface, decorated with raised patterns. Terracotta statuettes were placed on pedestals; in fact, everything spoke of luxury and comfort, but, alas, sorrow had found its way into the home and tears fell from Placidia's eyes, as she said over and over again: "My baby, my baby".

Felicius sat with set face watching her. Placidia had throughout her life been petted and spoilt, always getting her own way; now she was badly fitted to bear a trial which had befallen her, and which no coaxing or scolding could remedy.

"It is the uncertainty that appals me," she said. "If only I knew what had become of her. Felicius, we must never give up the search for her until she is found".

"No, indeed. The men have dragged the river, and there is no sign of the little one's body. Somehow, I distrust her nurse's word."

"Have you questioned her again? I cannot bear to see her," Placidia answered.

"Yes, I have examined her. She declares they were walking by the river and our little Julia ran in front of her and slipped into the water, that she waded in and tried to rescue her, but the current was too strong and the child was swept away. It is true that the woman's clothing was wet when she came back with the news, but the river is not swift here, it is a slow current. I do not believe her story."

Felicius did not tell his wife that it had been reported to him that the child's nurse had been seen gossiping with a young Roman soldier and it was rumoured that a band of British raiders had been in the neighbourhood. Felicius had his fears, and determined his men should search everywhere, the length and breadth of Britain if necessary, in order to find their youngest and greatly-loved child.

Suddenly, Placidia raised herself from the couch on which she had been lying, exclaiming "Felicius, one thing I am resolved on, the nurse shall die; crucifixion is too good for her."

Felicius looked grave.

"My wife", he said, "we must show mercy. I am thinking of the words I heard in Rome, 'Render to no man evil for evil. Avenge not yourselves.' Were we not told that the teaching of Christ was: 'Forgive men their trespasses'?"

Placidia shrugged her shoulders impatiently.

"Felicius, you are not one of the followers of the despised Nazarene, surely. I never felt it was wise for you to attend those gatherings in the catacombs; it was there you heard that letter written by their leader, Paul. But you, you are not Christian?"

"No, Placidia, I do not feel I am really one of them yet. I sometimes wish I were. I am influenced by their teaching and behaviour under persecution."

"If you encourage thoughts like these, forgiveness, mercy and such like, you will grow weak and unable to manage your men, I fear."

Felicius smiled.

"No, Placidia. The followers of the Christ are stronger than ordinary men, not weaker. Anyhow, my dear, I am absolutely determined that the poor, foolish woman shall not be punished as you suggest. I will try to get her to tell me the truth."

Placidia knew it was useless to argue with her husband when he spoke in such a resolute fashion and, at that moment, their older children entered, Marcus, a handsome lad of sixteen, Canace, aged ten, and Flora, four years old.

Canace and Flora had been crying; Canace in grief for her little sister and Flora because Canace cried; Marcus was grave and quiet.

Marcus put his arm around his mother saying, “Do not grieve, mother, we will never rest until we have found her.”

“How can we find her, if her body has been swept away into the sea, my son?” Placidia asked.

Marcus made no reply.

Later, when alone with his father, Marcus said: “Father, I have been questioning nurse. I knew she would be more likely to tell me the truth than anyone else. She admits that she lost sight of Julia and made up the story about the river. She waded into the water to wet her garments and make her tale seem true.”

Felicius replied, “Do not tell your mother this, my son. It will only cause her deeper unrest. Tomorrow, I will send off a band of soldiers to search, not returning until they have found Julia.”

Alas for Felicius’ plans! That very evening, a messenger arrived from Rome. Felicius was recalled to his native city. His royal master demanded an instant return; there must be no delay in obeying the imperial mandate, so all hope of finding Julia was abandoned for the time being.

But Felicius bent his knee in prayer, not to the gods of his forefathers, nor to any of the British deities, but to the One of whom he knew so little and yet in whom he was beginning to place his trust, asking that his little daughter might be kept from all harm, find friends to comfort her and, in God’s own time, be restored to her parents.

Chapter 6.

The Arrival Of Bernard

THE weeks passed uneventfully in the household of Cynvelin. Little Julia lost her frightened look and no longer said: "Julia wants her mother". She became happy in Venissa's care. Venissa was devoted to her and would probably have spoilt the child with undue indulgence had not Hulda interfered, making certain rules for the child's daily life and exacting obedience from her.

The only time the haunted look of terror re-appeared in Julia's eyes was whenever a Druidical priest came in sight. At such moments, Julia would run and hide in any available corner or bury her face in the folds of Hulda's or Venissa's gown, finding comfort in a sheltering arm. It was many days before Julia gained confidence in Cynvelin's presence; she evidently realised that it was a man who had been her captor and consequently feared all men, but Cynvelin's unfailing gentleness at last won her, and she would sit on his knee talking her pretty childish prattle.

Alaric soon became a favourite, for he was gifted in carving animals from blocks of wood and Julia was delighted with his gifts, especially when he made her a long-legged horse balanced on a curved piece of wood, so that it rocked.

One day, Julia stood looking at him with puzzled air and then said slowly: "Are you Marcus?"

Occasionally she spoke of Canace and Flora, but soon early memories died down and Julia forgot her people.

Hulda had given directions that the little woollen tunic, daintily embroidered, in which the child had been dressed when brought to them should be kept and, later, as her little arm grew too plump for the bangle, it was removed and stored with the tunic.

One morning, towards the end of the winter, Venissa was with her mother, busy with a hand loom. The warp was of plain, fawn-colour wool and Venissa was adding a woof in various shades, pushing each strand in place with a long wooden comb. On the floor beside her was a heap of wool of different colours, having been tinted with vegetable dyes, and Julia was passing the strands to her as she required them.

"Mother", she said, "shall I have a pattern of blue and yellow or green and brown to edge this material?"

Hulda considered, putting her head slightly on one side, a trick of hers when thinking.

"Green and brown, I think, dear, the colours seem to suit one another, I always think, perhaps because the woods are so tinted in the fall of the year."

Cynvelin, entering at that moment, stood admiring the scene; it was, he thought, a pretty sight and many would have agreed with him; Venissa, fair and dainty; Julia, dark and sparkling, while Hulda sat with motherly grace beside the young folk; the bright colours of the work adding charm to the picture. Cynvelin flung off his fur cloak, sat down on a low stool and stretched his legs towards the blazing logs that burnt cheerily on the hearth. He looked grave and Hulda asked: "Is anything the matter, dearest?"

"Only that poor old Griselda has gone."

"Gone! Do you mean she has left her hut?"

"No, dear. She was found this morning on the river path and had evidently been killed by a wild boar. The man who found her saw the spoor of the animal. I have sent the men to bury her; they were reluctant to obey, I could see. I believe one and all would risk my displeasure and severe punishment rather than go near the hut, so sure are they that the place is haunted and that the evil eye will fall on them, if found near the spot."

"Poor old Griselda. I wonder what has become of the cat," Venissa said. "Mother, with your permission, I would like to go and look for it. Alaric would accompany me, I am sure."

"You must wait for a fine morning, my child, then you may."

So when, next morning, the sun shone in a clear sky, Alaric and Venissa made their way along the river path and up the hill to the hut. No trace of the cat could be found; it had probably gone off to join the wild cats which abounded in the woods.

"I know what people will say," Alaric remarked, "that it was spirited away to join its mistress."

The two went into the hut and found everything in order; humble though it was, it was neat and clean; a stack of logs in the corner; rough woollen rugs and a sheep skin on the low couch; pots for stewing; a drinking-vessel stood by the hearth, while a store of honey, grain and nuts was on the shelf.

"I wonder who will be the next to live here," Venissa said; and Alaric answered, "Perhaps nobody. It will become a ruin after a time."

"Not for a long time, Alaric. It is very strongly built. Somehow I feel I should like to keep it in order. We could come here and light a fire sometimes."

"Of course, we can. It would not be a bad shelter for anyone, if needed," was Alaric's opinion.

With a last look around, the two shut the door and turned homeward.

Venissa walked in a thoughtful mood and, presently, Alaric said, "What are you thinking about, Venissa?"

"I was wondering about Griselda. Death is so mysterious. Where is she now?"

"Well, her body is under the ground, we know that."

"Yes, but the real Griselda, the something that made her what she was. You see, Alaric, we all have faces and hands, eyes and ears, but yet we are all different. There is something that makes us just ourselves and at death that something is gone, where?"

Alaric thought a minute or two, then said, "You know, Venissa, our priests tell us that the spirit never dies; it enters another body, so Griselda is somewhere."

"I suppose so, but we know so little. I hate the thought of death. Some time my father and mother will die; it comes to everyone in time."

"Don't think about it, Venissa. Anyhow your people are not old. Let us have a race and forget gloomy subjects."

Venissa, fleet of foot, was very willing, so off they went, slackening their pace as they drew near Venissa's home, for Hulda was particular about her daughter's behaviour.

At the gateway, they saw Cynvelin standing talking to a stranger.

"Look, Alaric, who is that old man, I wonder?" Venissa exclaimed.

The visitor was an elderly man with white hair and dark eyes; to Alaric and Venissa in their youthfulness he appeared extremely old.

"He may be a bard. I do hope so," Venissa added. "We have not had a visit from one for such a long time."

"He does not appear to have a cithara with him; he would have, if he were a bard," Alaric answered.

The young people hurried forward and Cynvelin said as they drew near: "This is my daughter, Venissa, and a young neighbour, Alaric; and this is Bernard, whom we shall be pleased to entertain."

Alaric, after greeting the newcomer politely, said goodbye, and Venissa accompanied her father and his guest into the house.

Presently, Venissa ventured to ask: "Are you a bard, sir?"

"No, little lady. I have not the gift of song. I am a saga-man."

"Oh, delightful!" Venissa answered. "Then will you tell us some stories?"

"Yes, indeed, with your gracious parents' permission. That is why I am here."

"And will it be a love story?"

Bernard smiled.

"Yes. I propose tomorrow to tell you the love story of Gladys, the daughter of our hero king, Caradoc ; then, on the next day, if I may be permitted, I want to tell you the greatest love story of all."

Venissa was quite excited. In fact, every one was pleased at the coming of Bernard. As Hulda remarked to her husband: "We must get all our neighbours together, for it is only by listening to the bards and saga-men that the history of our land can be made known and kept in the memory of our young people, that they in their turn will pass it on to the next generation."

Chapter 7.

An Old-Time Love Story.

NEXT day it seemed as though spring had come in earnest, the air was balmy, the sun shone and birds sang, altogether quite a suitable day for a gathering which was practically in the open air, for the large, covered-in space in Cynvelin's enclosure was without walls. It was with a sense of pleasurable anticipation that Cynvelin, Hulda, Venissa and many neighbours assembled.

Some sat on benches, some on stools, while the younger ones sat on rugs on the ground and, outside the enclosure, the slaves congregated, almost as eager to hear as their owners.

Bernard took his place at one end and every eye was fixed on him; there was no need to ask for the attention of his audience, that was an assured matter; even little Julia, who sat close to Venissa on a thick sheepskin rug, lifted her big black eyes and watched Bernard with interest.

"My lord Cynvelin, and my lady Hulda," Bernard began, "I thank you for your gracious welcome and for giving me the opportunity of telling you some of the history of our land. Today, I want to tell you of our hero, king Caradoc. Rather over a hundred years ago, in the year 43, that part of our land known as Siluria was governed by King Caradoc and, when the Romans under Aulus Plautius, landed on our shores, as with one voice our people pleaded with Caradoc to take the lead and defend them against the enemy. Plautius having landed at Rutupium, [4]. he marched along the great road Watling Street, which runs from Dover to Holyhead, constructed as doubtless some of you know by Dyfnval, over five hundred years ago. Plautius had not marched far before he was met by Caradoc and a battle fought, the Romans gaining some measure of victory. This was followed by other battles, sometimes one side gaining, sometimes the other, Caradoc continuing to hold his own against Plautius, Vespasian and Geta. Finally, Plautius sent to Rome for instructions and reinforcements. The emperor decided to come to our land himself."

Bernard here asked a question: "Can you imagine, I wonder, what the emperor brought with him to aid in the conquest of our unfortunate troops?"

Cynvelin smiled. He had heard this history before, but he made no answer and the young people waited with interest for Bernard to continue.

"The emperor," Bernard went on, "had heard of the great damage his men had received from the British chariots with their long sweeping scythes protruding on each side, and drawn by magnificent horses who fearlessly rushed on his soldiers. Now, the emperor knew that one thing only would turn back these horses, that one thing being the odour of elephants, so he brought a number of these animals with

[4] Between Thanet and Richborough.

him. When they came on to the battle field, the horses gave way and our king Caradoc was defeated.

Imagine the scene! Our brave warriors urging their noble steeds forward; the sudden pause, the distended nostrils, the inquiring sniff, as the unusual, obnoxious smell preceded the actual presence of the mighty beasts. Then the terror of the horses, refusing to yield obedience to their drivers, turning, fleeing, disaster following.

"However, Claudius, the emperor, was willing to make a treaty, stipulating that if the Britons paid tribute to Rome they should continue the native government, making their own laws, ruling as lieutenants of the Roman emperor. Aulus Plautius remained in Britain with his family, and here comes the part of my story which I promised our little lady, Venissa, should be told--the love story of Gladys."

"Many of my listeners will agree with me, out of their own experience, that love laughs at barriers of race or circumstances; it takes no count of conquered or conqueror. Caradoc's lovely young daughter, noted for her grace, wit and charm, whose praises poets delighted to sing, came in contact with Aulus Rufus Pudens, the son of Aulus Plautius and, from the start of their acquaintance, the love was mutual. The Roman father might object to the British girl; the British father might equally oppose his daughter being united to one of the dreaded Romans, but the two young folk plighted their troth, heedless of difficulties, and waited. Pudens, to speak of him by the name by which he was mostly known, was stationed in our land, at Regnum (Chichester). He was at that time an ardent worshipper of the gods, so much so, that he gave land for the site of a temple to be erected to Neptune and Minerva. As my older listeners doubtless know, peace lasted only for a brief time. Our sturdy and independent people considered the kings who consented to rule as lieutenants of the Roman emperor as traitors, and Caradoc once again led forth his soldiers to war, this time in this very district where we are, the south-west of our land.

It seemed for Pudens and Gladys, the death knell of their hopes, for here were the two fathers engaged in battle. Plautius marched against Caradoc. While the Roman Vespasian sought to land at Torbay, another Roman, Geta, with his legions, commenced to build fortress after fortress right across the country in order to make the southern part a Roman province. Fighting started, battle after battle was fought."

Bernard paused, looking round at his audience. He was content to see interest on every face, so continued:

"I will not weary you with a detailed recital of each battle. Caer Isca (Exeter) was besieged by Vespasian and while there he nearly lost his life, for he was taken unawares while in the trenches and would have been slain in his tent, had not his son, Titus, come unexpectedly on the scene and rescued his father from the hands of his captor. Every British man, from peasant to prince, was devoted to Caradoc, as well they might be, for he was a patriot of high degree, leading his army against the greatest military power in the world. Alas, bravery and a refusal to know when beaten were not sufficient to deliver our land from her foes! There came a day, at last, when the Romans gained a great victory. Caradoc's wife, daughters, Gladys and Eurgain, and his sons, three in number, all fell into enemy hands and were conveyed to the Roman camp at Uriconium (Wroxeter)."

Bernard's manner of speech was so impressive that when he spoke of the captivity of Gladys, Venissa involuntarily said:

"Oh-h!" and then flushed with shame at her impulsive interruption.

Bernard smiled at her and all felt the charm of his countenance.

"I am glad that my lady Venissa appreciates the reality of my tale, for it is no fairy story I tell, but the history of our land and, as such, I would want to have it remembered and, as occasion occurs, passed on to others. Possibly you can one and all imagine the state of Caradoc's mind, but worse was to follow. Cartismandua, queen of the Brigantes, whose land was in the north-east of Britain, had always told Caradoc that he could, in any time of need, find refuge at her court, so, at this moment, he took advantage of her invitation and fled to Eboracum (York). Caradoc had been a good friend to her in former days and now she received him cordially. It was not long before he, worn out with the stress of battle, retired to rest and slept soundly. It was evident that treachery ran as a hereditary taint in Cartismandua's blood for, in former history, a relative of hers had acted as traitor. Now, waiting until she saw that Caradoc's sleep was deep, she sent a message to the enemy and soon poor Caradoc was surrounded, bound in chains, and delivered to a Roman general."

A low groan broke from the lips of many of Bernard's listeners.

Bernard again took up his story: "Tidings were sent to Rome, and instruction received that Caradoc and his entire family were to be sent to that city. Caradoc, his wife, two daughters, the Princes Eurgain and the Princess Gladys, his sons, Cyllinus Lleyn (or Linus) and Cynon, also Caradoc's father Brennus, were all taken to Rome."

Bernard ceased speaking for a moment, an expression came into his eyes that rather puzzled the more thoughtful members of his audience. It was a look of triumph, and yet he had spoken of defeat and captivity. He seemed to have forgotten his listeners, for his face was upturned and he murmured, "Great God, Thou makest the wrath of man to praise Thee and workest all things for good."

"Please do tell us what became of Gladys," Venissa said, and Bernard replied: "All in good time, little lady. What was I saying? Ah! Yes, I remember. Caradoc and his family were taken captive to Rome, the most wonderful city in the world. When Caradoc saw the great buildings he said: 'It is indeed strange that a people possessed of such magnificence at home should envy me my soldier's tent in Britain.' It seemed, of course, inevitable that the whole family would perish. It was the custom in Rome that important captives should march through the city in chains, and, reaching a certain spot, be cast into the Tarpein dungeons and either starved to death or killed, the bodies being cast into the Tiber.

Unaccountable as it seems, Caradoc and his family were not treated in this fashion; clemency was shown to them. Was it through the influence of Pudens who, in his love for Gladys, doubtless left no stone unturned to secure her safety and that of her relations; or was it because of the report that the Britons were again gaining victories in their country? For, after the capture of Caradoc, or Caractacus as the Romans named him, the Romans were put to flight again and yet again. Possibly it appeared to the Roman authorities that cruelty to

Caradoc might lead to deeper suffering for their Roman army and civilians in Britain. Be that as it may, Caradoc was allowed to plead his cause before the tribunal of the emperor. After being marched through the city, where thousands of people blocked the procession in their desire to obtain a glimpse of so important a captive, Caradoc took his place before the emperor and spoke with composure.

'Had my government in Britain been directed solely with a view to the preservation of my hereditary domains or the aggrandisement of my own family, I might long since have entered this city as an ally, not a prisoner; nor would you have disdained for a friend, a king descended from illustrious ancestors, and the dictator of many nations. My present condition, stripped of its former majesty, is as adverse to myself as it is the cause of triumph to you. What then? I was lord of men, horses, wealth, arms; what wonder if, at your dictation, I refused to resign them? Does it follow that because the Romans aspire to universal dominion, every nation is to accept the vassalage they would impose? I am now in your power—betrayed, not conquered. Had I like others yielded without resistance, where would have been the name of Caradoc, and where your glory? Oblivion would have buried both in the same tomb. Bid me live, I shall survive for ever in history one example at least of Roman clemency.' "

Once again, Bernard paused in his speech; many who were listening spellbound heaved a sigh. Alaric's eyes glistened, as did the eyes of most of the young people. Caradoc's appealing speech moved them greatly. A longing to be similarly heroic stirred in their hearts. They were impatient for Bernard to continue that they might hear what was the response of the Roman emperor to Caradoc's brave words.

Bernard did not keep them waiting long but continued: "Strange to say, the emperor was induced to spare the lives of Caradoc and his family. The conditions were that Caradoc—remember his name was Latinised to Caractacus—was never to bear arms against Rome again and to reside in Rome for seven years. He was allowed to receive the revenues from the royal Silurian [5]. domains. The beauty and charm of

[5] Siluria being the part of Briton over which Caradoc ruled.

Caradoc's daughter, Gladys, so affected the emperor that he announced that henceforth she was to be treated as his adopted daughter and receive the name of Claudia, his family name, and, more than that, he was pleased to approve the betrothal between her and Pudens. So that, in the end, true love triumphed and the marriage was celebrated in the year 53. Two of Caradoc's sons returned to Britain, Cyllinus succeeded his father as king of Siluria, while the third Lleyn, or Linus, remained with his father."

Bernard had apparently finished. Some one asked: "Is that the end?"

"No, it was the beginning," Bernard answered, and some murmured: "How could that be?" "It was the beginning of new life for many.

While in Rome the family of Caradoc learnt the one true religion and, when Brennus, the father of Caradoc, his grand-daughter Eurgain, Caradoc's elder daughter, and others came back to our land they brought with them a knowledge of the one true God and Saviour and bore witness to what they had learnt of Christ. Many heard that story, the greatest love story ever told, and, with your permission, sir," Bernard turned to Cynvelin, "I will relate it to you tomorrow."

Cynvelin signified his willingness to hear what Bernard had to tell them and thanked him for the interesting hour they had spent. Bernard returned the compliment by thanking his listeners for the complete attention they had given to him.

Chapter 8.

Good News.

"CYNVELIN," Hulda said to her husband, when they were by themselves later in the day, "Cynvelin, did you understand the saga-man's allusion to the one true God? What did he mean?"

"It appeared to me that he is the proclaimer of some new strange god, but we shall know more tomorrow," Cynvelin answered.

"Do you think it wise, my husband, to allow him free speech? We do not want strange ideas put into the minds of our young people, nor can we risk offending our own gods. It makes me feel afraid."

Hulda was timid and in bondage to the gods of her fore-fathers.

"Do not be fearful, my love, there is no harm in hearing what Bernard has to say; it need not disturb our belief or worship. Each nation has its own gods and Bernard has travelled much and probably came under the influence of some foreign god. You know, I have heard that Brennus, Eurgain and others adopted a new religion, but we are firmly settled in our worship and shall not be easily swayed, although I must admit that Bernard has a strange persuasive manner and a great charm; however, it would take more than that to make me change my religion; what was good enough for my fathers is good enough for me."

Hulda sighed. "Religion is a terrible thing, Cynvelin; at least, ours is, so cruel, so grasping. One never knows when our priests may say the gods require a sacrifice and our dearest may be demanded."

Hulda shuddered, and Cynvelin put his arm around her; but he had no word of comfort for her. What she had said was only too true. He sought to turn her thoughts into another channel.

"Well, it is a good thing the old time of war and bloodshed is over. The Roman occupation has turned out to be beneficial for our land and for us all. Look at the roads they have made; what trades they have introduced! Why, when I visited Calleva Atrebation (Silchester), I was amazed at the buildings and the trades. The city is surrounded by a wall from fifteen feet to twenty-one feet in height, nine to fifteen feet in thickness; it has four gateways and, outside, are suburbs where there are rose gardens of great beauty. There are shops, wine merchants, fish sellers, poulterers and others. Their physicians are very clever and the beauty specialists for the women are truly remarkable."

Cynvelin laughed and went on,

"I am thankful to say our women are beautiful enough without so many aids. You, my dear Hulda, and our Venissa need no colouring for your faces, nor all the other fanciful things the Roman ladies consider necessary. But I must admit their villas were indeed magnificent, most luxurious, and their baths are a wonderful sight."

"And what gods do they worship?" Hulda asked.

"Oh, various gods, as we do. Mercury, Venus, Jupiter, but, at the entrance to one villa, I saw a strange character carved on stone. I was told it was two Greek letters χ and ρ forming, in combination, the first two letters of a new god and, when I come to think of it, I believe it was the name Bernard mentioned yesterday: 'Christ.'"

"Cynvelin, is it a true report that the Romans have suppressed the Druids in many places in our land and forbidden human sacrifices? I almost wish they would do the same here."

"No, no, Hulda, do not wish that. Remember if we fear the gods, they do protect us from many evils. It is true that the Romans have put down the Druids, and I can quite understand their motives, for our priests say it is patriotism to seek to stir up the young people to a spirit of rebellion against the Romans, and in many places the Druids prevent a peaceful occupation. However, here I think my influence prevents trouble. On the one hand, I give my protection to the Druids and, on the other hand, I encourage my people in obedience to the laws of the Romans, for they have introduced much that is for our good: a high state of civilisation, new methods of trading and many other useful things."

While Cynvelin and Hulda were talking, Bernard was making friends with Venissa and Julia. Julia was Venissa's shadow and was never, if she could help it, separated from the one who had been so kind to her.

"Will you please tell me what became of Gladys, or should I say, Claudia?" Venissa asked. "Do you know anything more about her?"

"Claudia is the name by which she was always known during the latter part of her life and by which she will go down to posterity. I can tell you a little more of her. She had four children, Timotheus, Novatus, Pudentiana and Praxedes. A poet, Martial, sang her praises and wrote of her that which he evidently considered high praise:

'Though Claudia from the sea-green Britons came,
She wears the aspect of a Roman dame.'

Her husband, Pudens, was a wealthy man; his establishment consisted of about four hundred servants. Claudia wrote several hymns, and in her home she welcomed many followers of Christ. She, Pudens, and her four children each won a martyr's crown, while Caradoc, Cyllenus and Eurgain died natural deaths in this our land."

Venissa failed to understand all Bernard said.

“A martyr’s crown”, it was puzzling, but the time was yet to come when Venissa would herself understand the true meaning of these mysterious words. Now she asked: “Who is Christ?”

Before Bernard could reply, Hulda came into the room and the conversation was interrupted, except that Bernard said: “I will try to explain to you tomorrow, when I tell you the greatest love story ever told.”

Next day, Bernard looked round on his audience with great interest. There were young folk present with keen eyes and eager faces; there were some there with indifferent, bored expressions; others old and drooping, and not a few with sad, worn, weary countenances. Among the latter was Osmond’s mother, Elfrida. Bernard’s attention was particularly drawn to her; her face told its own story of sorrow. Although he did not know the history of her life, yet he felt sure here was a soul needing comfort. Had he known of the sacrifice of her precious daughter, Ida, in the past, to please the gods as the priests told her and, now, the giving up of her son to leave home for training as a priest, a process which she knew in many cases seemed to deaden all human affection, and which left her home desolate, Bernard would not have marvelled at the expression of suffering stamped on the woman’s face.

Bernard began slowly: “Friends, this morning I watched from yonder hill the rising of the sun, a beautiful spectacle as it gradually came into sight, and I was not surprised to see one figure after another prostrate himself or herself in worship before the majestic orb. Similarly, tonight you will do the same in adoration of the moon. You worship the sun, the moon, but have you ever asked yourself who is it that makes the sun to rise and set, never too early or too late, but at its appointed time? Who is it that controls the waxing and the waning of the moon; that causes the bud to shoot on the tree? Look around now. The mighty oak looks lifeless, but you know that in a short time buds will form and presently the oak will be dressed in verdant green. You worship the oak; you worship and fear many gods; you *fear* them, I say, for you think that all evil, all disasters, come from the gods whom you may have all unwittingly offended. I have come to tell you of the great God Who created the sun, the moon; Who makes the oak to bud and Who--listen, is a God of love."

A little gasp seemed to come from many in the audience: "A God of love!" Never had such tidings reached them.

Bernard continued. "God is loving and desires to put peace into your hearts in place of fear. I can tell that many of you are strangers to peace; you are worried, anxious, terror-stricken, but of peace you know nothing. The One of Whom I speak says: 'Come unto Me, and I will give you rest.' But while I tell you that God is love, I must also tell you that God is holy and righteous, and God has said: 'The soul that sinneth it shall die.' That is the sentence that God has passed upon man. Let me ask you, have you ever sinned? Have you ever done that which is wrong? Have you not deserved the wrath of a Holy God? I want each one of you to look back over your life and ask yourself the question and answer it to yourself. Have you done that which is evil ?"

There was a great stillness while Bernard waited awhile. His heart was lifted up in prayer that God would give a spirit of conviction to many souls. Some fidgeted; some heads drooped as he waited; faces were grave.

"Have you recalled that evil thing you did to another? Has your heart spoken? Do you remember that deceit you practised and thought yourself clever because you were not found out? Are you recalling that lie which you told? All these things are sins, sins against the God Who, although He loves you, can never pass over your wrong doings. Again, I repeat the words: 'The soul that sinneth it shall die.' Are there some here that are saying: ' We will not do these things again, we will seek to please this great God?' But that resolution does not alter the sentence, does not put away your past sins. What can be done? Listen, I have more to tell you. God has found a way out of the difficulty. A way whereby man may be pardoned and sin blotted out. God's beloved Son, Jesus Christ, came down to this world, He lived among men, blessing and healing many, and then He gave His life to make an atonement for sin. We deserved to suffer the penalty for our own sins, but Christ, God's Son, willingly bore the punishment for sinners that they might be pardoned and forgiven."

Bernard stopped and some of them thought that he had finished speaking to them.

One or two spoke eagerly, among them Elfrida.

"Can you not tell us more? Make us understand it. It is so new to us to hear of a God who loves us. We cannot take it in."

Satisfied that he had roused the interest of at least some of those who sat around him, Bernard continued: "When God created this world, He made a man and woman and placed them in a beautiful garden where they lived in happiness and peace, without sin. Then, one day, the evil one, whom we call Satan, came. He tempts men to do wrong, and he tempted the man and woman to disobedience and man fell. That was the beginning of sin, the sin which shuts man out from the presence of a loving but just God. At once there was a separation between God and man, but God promised to send a Saviour to bring man back to God. Long years passed, man sinned again and yet again. Then, one day, Christ Jesus, God's own Son, came into this world, as I told you just now. He dwelt in a baby form, grew to manhood, bringing blessing to all who sought His help; but man, wicked man hated the Light that His words brought, they loved darkness and evil, and, presently, they took Him and condemned Him to death. The Christ Who had walked their streets, the One Who had spoken words of comfort, Who had fed the hungry ones, healed the sick, taken the little children in His arms and blessed them, Him they hated and sought to kill. When the time had come that He was to lay down His life, to bear the penalty for sinners, to make reconciliation between fallen man and God, He allowed them to take Him, to scourge Him, to crucify Him. And, when He had accomplished a complete and full sacrifice for sin, He yielded up His Spirit and died on the Cross."

"Was that the end?" a voice asked.

"No, no; indeed! They took Him down from the Cross, laid Him in a tomb, making it fast with a mighty stone but, after three days, the Christ, the Saviour, arose from the grave. He was seen by His followers, talked with them, blessed them, and then returned to His Father Who had sent Him, Who so loved the world that He gave His only begotten Son to die. And now, He lives; He lives on high; He hears us when we talk to Him; He forgives us when we confess our sins; He loves us today. Will you not seek Him? Will you not ask Him to forgive you; to make you His own? We will now speak to Him and He will hear us."

Bernard then prayed, a simple prayer that many of his hearers could follow with understanding.

After this, the gathering broke up, each going their separate ways and then, as always, there was a vast difference in the hearts of those who scattered. Some were strangely moved, desirous of hearing more; some were scornful and even angry; many were indifferent and returned to their occupations, forgetting what they had heard, feeling more interest in the story of Claudia and Pudens which Bernard had told them the previous day.

Among those who were interested was Elfrida. The words: "Come unto Me and I will give you rest," lingered in her mind. Rest! How she longed for it! She determined to seek Bernard again and hear more of the One Who could give rest to her poor, tempest-tossed soul.

Cynvelin was thoughtful. Bernard's words had given him food for thought. He could not lightly dismiss them from his mind; rather, they seemed to him to meet a long-felt need, but he was not one to form an opinion swiftly; he would think over what he had heard, question Bernard on one or two points and be thoroughly convinced before accepting this new teaching.

Venissa and Alaric were greatly stirred; Venissa not so much by the words she had heard, but because of the light that shone on Bernard's face.

She said to Alaric, later in the day: "Alaric, did you notice how happy Bernard looked? His eyes were shining, and—and—I cannot describe it, but it was a look I had never seen on any face before."

"Yes, indeed, I did see it, Venissa. Do you know, Venissa, it is just what I have been thinking lately, that there must be something better for us than the religion of cruelty that we know? I have often stood on the hill and listened to the birds singing, looked at the sunshine, heard the rustle of the breeze among the leaves, and thought how beautiful it all is, and wondered if the Someone who made all this did not mean us to be happy and good."

"Alaric, I did not know you had such beautiful thoughts. How lovely it would be if every one was like Bernard; if only everyone could know about Christ and love Him. I feel I am beginning to love Him already. It was so good of Him to die for sinners. Don't you think so, Alaric?"

Alaric hesitated.

"I feel I want to think about it, Venissa, I don't seem to take in that part of it. I like to think there is a God Who loves us, but I'm not sure that we are all sinners. You are not, for one."

"Oh, Alaric! I felt when Bernard was speaking that I had done lots of wrong things and a sort of feeling inside that even if I had not done a lot of wrong, yet my heart is bad anyhow."

Alaric made no reply for a moment then he said: "I wonder what the priests will say to this?"

"Don't you think they will be glad to hear that there is a God Who is not cruel? One Whom we may love and not dread? One Who does good and wants us to know rest and peace?" Venissa asked.

Alaric laughed.

"Not likely, Venissa. Don't you see, if we all believed this, their power over us would be broken, and the Druids love power more than any thing else? They will be furious, I think, and Bernard will need to look to his own safety."

"I am sorry. I hoped they would be glad to hear the good news," Venissa answered.

Chapter 9.

An Old Disciple's Death.

"FATHER, are you going to the catacombs for the meeting tonight?" said Marcus to his father, Felicius.

Felicius started. He had scarcely realised that his son knew of the secret gatherings, and certainly had not dreamed that the lad was interested.

"Why do you ask, my son?" Felicius inquired.

"Father, I should like to accompany you, for I should like to confess my faith in Christ."

For a moment Felicius was speechless.

"My boy," he said at last, "I cannot understand this. What do you know of Christ?"

"Why, father, you yourself have told me of Him, and how wonderful His life and teaching were, and how He died for us on the cross, but I have learnt more from Sigma."

"Sigma, your mother's slave! Is she a Christian?"

"Yes, father. I had often wondered at her patience and cheerfulness and, a few months ago, not long after we arrived here from Britain, I came into my mother's room and heard my mother command Sigma to cast some incense on the altar she has in her room in honour of Vesta. Sigma said, quite respectfully: 'I pray you to excuse me, lady. I worship the one true God and I cannot sacrifice to a false god!' My mother was very angry and she hit Sigma on her face again and again until the poor woman's face bled. I could not help noticing how, although tears came into Sigma's eyes, yet there was a look of radiance on her face. Later in the day, I sought her and asked why she seemed happy in spite of her disgrace and suffering. For I knew, as my mother's chief attendant, she would feel dishonoured at being punished when several of the younger slaves were present."

"And what did she tell you, Marcus?" Felicius asked.

"She said, 'My heart leaped for joy, because I was called to suffer for my Master's sake Who had suffered so much for me.' I could not understand what she meant at first, and I said: 'My father, Felicius, is your master, has he suffered for you?' She answered: 'Felicius is my earthly master and a good master he is, but Jesus Christ is my Heavenly Master, my Saviour, my Lord, my Shepherd, and He knows now that I love Him, for I have suffered for His sake.' "

"I am surprised, Marcus, at what you tell me. I thought her a poor, ignorant slave woman and yet she knows more than I do. What else did she tell you?"

"A great deal, Sir. She was brought up in Smyrna and was taught in her young days by a man called Polycarp, who knew a wonderful man, called John, who was one of the disciples of Christ; so Sigma is able to tell me much about the Saviour and what she has told me has made me love Him. At first, when she told me of His holiness, of His words which condemn sin, I felt in despair, but then, Sigma told me that it was said of Him, 'This Man receiveth sinners,' and that He lives today and still welcomes the sinner and forgives and cleanses from sin. I came to Him, father and, oh! father, I know in my heart that He has received me, so now I want to confess Him."

Felicius' head was bowed.

"My boy, you make me feel ashamed. For some years I have been in touch with those who love and serve the Saviour; in my heart I believe in Him, and yet I have been too fearful to declare myself a Christian. I have tried to carry out the teaching of the Christ, and I absent myself from the public worship of the idols but, you know, Marcus, your mother is a devout worshipper of the gods, Vesta, Diana and the *lares* and *penates,* our household gods. She refuses to listen to anything I would tell her of Christ, and I fear I have let my love for her influence me."

"Father, let us go together to the meeting tonight and make our confession."

Felicius still hesitated.

"Marcus, my son, do you realise the peril? The followers of Christ have ever been persecuted. The list of the names of the martyrs is a long one; young and old, men and women alike, have suffered, been cast to the lions, burnt, crucified. I tremble for you."

"Father, do not fear. We may not be called to lay down our lives for Him. He may want us to live and serve Him; but even if it should be as you fear, will not the Saviour give us grace? Sigma told me of one who suffered for Christ—one Paul, who wrote: 'The Lord stood by me and strengthened me.' "

"Yes, my son, doubtless you are right. I, too, have heard of this man Paul. It was he who wrote the letter to the Christians here in Rome, which we have read at our gatherings. It is a wonderful epistle; some of the words I can never forget. He wrote: 'God commended His love toward us, in that while we were yet sinners, Christ died for us.' These words have lingered in my mind and brought me joy on many occasions. God's love, Christ's death, for us. You spoke of Polycarp, my son. I have often heard of him; he still lives, and he is a faithful witness for Christ."

Felicius sat a while, lost in thought, and Marcus waited. Presently, his father spoke again:

"Well, my son, if you really wish to come with me tonight to the Catacombs, you may do so. You are not a child now; you are old enough to make a decision for yourself, and I would not hold you back from following the Master, but I could wish we were back in Britain. It is easier to witness for Christ there than here for, although the Druids hate Christianity, we are their masters in that land and they dare not interfere with us but, I fear, if any of their own people confess Christ, they suffer."

"You may be sent there again, Father, and then we could start afresh to search for our little Julia."

Felicius sighed at the mention of his daughter, and Marcus continued: "Thank you for your permission to accompany you tonight. At what time do we start?"

"Not until dark. I will send Laon to summon you to join me at the right moment."

"Does Laon come with us?"

"Yes ; he is to be trusted. I am not sure that he is a Christian, but he has served me since I was a child, and his affection is great for me."

"All the slaves love you, Father, and they have reason to do so."

When darkness fell, Marcus awaited his father's summons with eagerness. His feelings were somewhat mixed. There was a longing to join with those who worshipped the Saviour Whom he had learnt to love, and yet he could not but remember that he and his father were running a great risk. Christians were cast to the lions to provide amusement for pleasure-loving, heartless men and women in Rome in those days, and Marcus knew it well; but he prayed for courage before they started and set out with his father with triumphant joy in his heart. They went first through the grounds which surrounded their villa, walking noiselessly in the shade of the holly trees, until they came out into the high road, passing the many fountains that adorned the road, hearing the splash and the ripple of the water, as the fountains sent up their spray, falling among the marble nymphs, cherubs, naiads, dolphins or youths with which they were decorated and gracefully ornamented. Then they came to the Via Appia and, finally, reached the entrance to the catacombs [6]. and went down a sloping passage to the underground.

Marcus had never been there before, and he looked round with interest. Torches were lit and, in their light, he saw tier after tier where lay the bodies of the saints. Here and there was a carved fish. Marcus knew it was the Christian symbol, the Greek word *Ichthus*, containing the initial letters of 'Jesus Christ, the Son of God, our Saviour.'

In other places, there were more elaborate carvings, the most frequent being that of a shepherd with a lamb on his shoulder. Marcus noticed, too, a standing figure of a man with hands extended in the attitude of prayer, and a vine with clusters of grapes moulded in plaster.

But Marcus' interest was soon transferred from the inanimate objects around to the group of people already gathered in the catacombs. There were men and women, old as well as those in the prime of life, several young men and a few maidens. The light from the torches, fixed in iron grips in the walls, fell on eager faces, all grouped around a man of about thirty-five years of age. He had arrived only a few moments before Felicius and Marcus, and an old man on the edge of the crowd said in a low tone to Felicius: "It is Irenaeus. He has recently come from Smyrna and he brings us news of Polycarp." Marcus was eager to hear, for had not Sigma told him of Polycarp, and Marcus, although he had never met the old disciple, felt that he loved him, for Sigma had spoken of his saintliness in such terms that Marcus' youthful affection had been stirred.

What was Irenaeus saying? The words fell like a thud of doom on their ears.

"Polycarp has gone to the Master Whom he loved and served."

---

[6] The place of sleeping. The name "Catacomb" was not given until the third century. These were tunnels hewn out by the early Christians as repositories for their dead and used as safe places for their meetings for worship, for the Romans honoured burial places; although later, in the third century, even there the Christians were not safe from their enemies, so secret entrances were made with clues impossible for an outsider to trace.

"Gone!"

Several voices spoke at once.

"How? When? Where?" they asked.

"He has won the martyr's reward and crown," was the answer.

"Alas! alas! Tell us how it happened. We thought he was in safety."

"Yes, so we all thought, for he had gone to a quiet country spot; all those who loved him had persuaded him to go away from Smyrna, that he might be out of danger and the reach of his enemies. Persecution has broken out in the city of late, and eleven of our little group of Christians have been thrown to the lions. This happened at the Annual Games, which were held in the huge stadium outside the town. Not content with this sacrifice, the people began to demand that our leader should be found and killed, but they could not find him and the people seemed to grow more and more determined to capture and torture those who refused to worship their false gods. The cry of 'away with the atheists' was heard on every side."

"Is that what they call the true believers, the followers of Christ?" one asked.

"Yes. In their ignorance they term us thus," Irenaeus continued. "We hoped Polycarp would not be found, but one day they took a young slave boy who knew where Polycarp was living and, although the poor lad stood firm in his refusal to disclose our leader's whereabouts for a long time, they tortured him so horribly that he let slip the name of the village. Possibly he hardly knew what he was saying in his great pain."

A low groan broke from the lips of Irenaeus' hearers.

Irenaeus continued his sad story.

"One night, not long ago, the soldiers arrived to take Polycarp. He greeted them politely, ordered food for them and, while they took a meal, he retired to his room for prayer, saying: 'The will of God be done.' Then, in consideration for his extreme old age, they mounted him on a donkey, and so accomplished the journey to Smyrna. Just before reaching the town, they were met by Herod, the Irenarch, and his father, Nicetus, who took him into their chariot and tried to persuade him to say, ' Caesar is Lord,' and to promise to burn incense to the idols. Finally, he reached the Stadium which, although immense, was crowded with spectators. The Proconsul, Titus, in spite of being a pagan, seemed moved to take pity on our leader's white head, and entreated him, as Herod had done, to hail Caesar as Lord. 'Renounce Christ, and you shall be free,' Titus urged.

'Eighty and six years have I served Christ. How can I deny the One Who saved me? How can I blaspheme my Saviour?' Polycarp answered.

The people shouted: 'Away with him to the lions; away with the father of the Christians.' But Titus refused to send him to the lions, saying: 'The games are over now.' But, finally, he yielded to the spectators and consented that Polycarp, our beloved minister, the aged servant of our Lord, should be burned alive."

Irenaeus paused, his voice choked with emotion. The faces turned to him were sad indeed; tears filled many eyes, for some knew Polycarp personally, and all had heard of his beautiful life and words of power.

Irenaeus continued: "The people were so filled with hate that they would brook no delay; they collected at once anything they could lay hands on that was combustible, even breaking up furniture and, making a stake, they bound the dear old saint to it. Still Polycarp prayed, thanking God that he was thought worthy of that day and hour to drink of Christ's cup of suffering, and praising God for the mercies of his life."

"Did he suffer long?" someone asked.

"No, at the last, an executioner was sent to kill him with the sword, and his life-blood quenched the flames. Now let us praise God that His servant is safe in His keeping, and let us pray that we who are left, may be kept true to His name and have grace to suffer, if such be His will for us."

After a time of prayer, Irenaeus read the Word of God and gave a helpful address. The opportunity was then given to those who had not already made confession of their faith to do so. Felicius and Marcus, among others, witnessed to the saving grace of God, and the hearts of those assembled were greatly cheered.

The young converts were exhorted to continue in the faith and told that, after a time of probation, they would be received into the fellowship of the Church by baptism.

Chapter 10

The Druids' Conference.

ALARIC was right in thinking Leirwg and the other priests would be furious at the teaching of Bernard, all the more because many were receiving his words with joy.

They met in conference to discuss the situation. The conference was held at one of their sacred spots in the depths of the forest; far, they thought, from listening ears.

Leirwg presided, and made the opening speech.

"Brothers," he said, "we are met here today to consider the menace to our religion introduced by this man Bernard. He has been in our midst many months, entertained by Cynvelin and his wife, Hulda. He draws the people around him, preaching this religion which is in opposition to all our teaching and practice. Not only does he seek to propound his ideas in the large congregation but he is visiting among the people and giving individual attention to many. At first I treated the matter with scorn; I felt our power over both rich and poor, bond and free, was such that his words would be of no avail, but I cannot but confess that this man has a subtle something about him which I cannot explain but which, I see, is winning many converts to his religion. His words have force, and numbers are accepting his doctrine and turning away from us. I shall be glad to hear from some of you what, in your opinion, is to be our attitude to this state of affairs. I will reserve my own ideas until later. I wish to hear yours."

One priest rose, and said: "I have been absent from this neighbourhood recently, as you all know; all this is news to me. I should like to know who has embraced this new religion."

Several names were mentioned; among others, Cynvelin; his daughter, Venissa; her friend, Alaric; also Elfrida.

An old priest then spoke: "Friends," he said, "we cannot but confess that this religion has power. To take one case only, I have been watching Elfrida, the mother of our young priest, Osmond. We all know how sad, how fearful, how despondent she was; now, she is completely changed; a strange peace has fallen upon her; a great courage has taken hold of her. When I spoke to her and reproved her for her lack of zeal in failing to be present at our last festival and gathering for worship, I expected to receive an apology from her and a promise for better conduct in the future. Instead, she spoke out boldly and said she no longer worshipped false gods but worshipped and served the one true God, Who gave His Son, Christ Jesus, to die for her sins and redeem her from the power of the enemy."

A low growl of anger, rising to a shout of passion, broke from the assembly at the name of Christ. Men, whose faces had been coldly passive a few moments before, became distorted with rage, and many spoke at once.

Leirwg called them to order. His strong face was immovable; he was not easily roused to anger, but was one who, with calm, relentless determination, and in cold blood, could carry out an action of intense cruelty, or plan and wait for some opportunity of revenge, rejoicing in its fulfilment in due course.

"Finish your remarks," he said, addressing the old priest who had been interrupted.

"I have not much more to say; only to point out that we have to realise that this is a religion of power; it will not be easily suppressed. Can you account for the fact that Elfrida is changed from a woman who could be terrorised into obeying any command of ours, even to the sacrificing of her daughter, Ida, and the yielding up of her son, Osmond; changed, I say, into a fearless woman and, more than that, into a happy one, too? She is upheld by a power which we cannot explain but with which we shall have to reckon. She is not the only one transformed. Look at young Alaric; wanting only to enjoy life, careless of others, formerly; what has he done recently? Spent hours in caring for an old, broken-down slave, who was cast out to die as useless. Alaric carried him into a hut on his father's estate, dressed his wounds, fed him, and cared for him until he died. More than that, he taught the poor, old creature this strange new belief and, through its power, he no longer feared death. I happened to look in at the hut just before he died; his face was radiant; he seemed unconscious of my presence but appeared to see some other person invisible to my poor eyes, for he said, over and over again: 'Saviour, Thou art with me. Thy love has taken away my fear. Thy blood has cleansed my sins away.' I lingered and listened, and the old slave died murmuring, 'Saviour.' What he meant I do not know, but I was conscious of a great peace in that little hut and as wonderful a change in him as in Elfrida."

The old priest ceased, and one man said angrily: "It seems to me you have accepted this accursed doctrine. You are one of them!"

"No," the old man said sadly. "No, I am old. Long have I served and worshipped the gods of our nation; now I am too old to change. It is not that I have accepted this teaching but that I see we need to realise it is a religion that has great power in the lives of those who have believed it, and I believe they would rather die than give it up."

"Well, then, they shall die," said one with grim determination.

"Not so fast, my brother," Leirwg interrupted. "We can afford to wait. Our plans must be laid carefully. We have to remember things are not as they were a hundred years ago; the good old days are past. Since the Roman occupation, we have to move with caution. Here in Devon we have been left much to our own devices, but it is not so in many parts of Britain; the Romans have suppressed our brethren, forbidden our sacrifices, even substituting the priests themselves, releasing those who were to have been offered to the gods."

"Why do they oppose us? They themselves have their own gods which they worship; why should they not allow us ours?" asked a young priest.

"Because they know it is we who keep alive the old patriotic spirit in the people. It is we who foster rebellion against our conquerors. I have heard that the Roman centurions say there will be no perfect safety for themselves and their soldiers until we are wiped out. So we must proceed with caution. My idea is this, that Bernard must be got rid of; when he is gone, the people will soon forget his teaching and be brought into order and subjection again. Failing this, we shall have to excommunicate one or two as an example to the others. That will put terror into them, and we shall regain our power."

"Yes, indeed," many murmured, for all knew the horror of excommunication. It was practically a death sentence, for no one dare give or sell food to the one thus sentenced; no one would give shelter to, nor employ, such a one, and the struggle for existence ended in either a slow death from starvation and exposure, or the weakened victim fell a prey to wild beasts.

Leirwg continued his remarks.

"Another reason for caution I must point out. We do not wish to offend our lord Cynvelin; he is our chief and Bernard is his guest. Therefore, I propose that one of our number be appointed to watch Bernard's movements and, if possible, gain his confidence; then, when we know that Bernard intends visiting some outlying village, as he does at times, we can be ready and —" the priest paused, "there is no need for me to explain. Bernard will be missing."

One or two applauded and, in the noise they made, no one noticed a slight rustle in a clump of bushes nearby. A young man who had hidden there had seized the opportunity of extricating himself from the thicket and slipping off without attracting attention to himself.

Alaric, that morning, had gone to the moor with bow and arrow, intent on hunting game. Not getting any success, he had wandered farther than usual and found himself in the distant forest. While there, voices had attracted his attention and, pausing to listen, he caught the name of Bernard. This aroused his interest and slowly, with great caution, he had crept near, hiding behind sheltering bushes and tangled undergrowth until, within a few yards of the priests, he was just in time to hear Leirwg's concluding remarks.

"Thank God," Alaric murmured to himself when once more he was well on the way home. "Thank God; my footsteps were guided this morning. Now, I must warn Bernard, and think out some plan for his safety."

Chapter 11

Hulda's Pleading

ALTHOUGH the priests under Leirwg, the Arch-Druid, thought they knew his plans and enjoyed his confidence, they were in reality greatly mistaken. He was of a subtle disposition, and preferred to act independently of his brethren. Moreover, he loved power; he delighted to feel he could sway the common people at will; to know that they trembled at the thought of his anger and would obey his command without questioning, gave him pleasure.

At the breaking up of the conference, he walked home alone deep in thought. No one watching him would have guessed at the depth of his feelings and the varying emotions that stirred his heart, for his face gave no sign. His thoughts chiefly centred round Cynvelin and his family. It was a matter of intense annoyance to him that he had lost his hold on Cynvelin. Formerly, the chief had conformed to the practices and rites of the Druidical religion without hesitation or demur, and had been a generous supporter of all Leirwg's schemes. The money Cynvelin had offered, at frequent intervals, to secure the goodwill of the gods for himself and his household, had been a source of income to Leirwg, a source which he had considered permanently secure. Now, it had failed. Cynvelin had lost all faith in the gods, and all fear too; consequently, Leirwg's hold over him was broken. Leirwg was secretly furious and he determined that Cynvelin should suffer. He would rather have pronounced the sentence of excommunication on Cynvelin with all the curses that accompanied it. How Leirwg would have rejoiced to have brought Cynvelin before the company of priests; to have struck his name off the roll of the book of his tribe; to have broken his sword; branded his forehead and proclaimed: "This man hath no name, nor family, nor tribe among the names and families of Britain; henceforth, let no man's flesh touch his flesh, nor tongue speak to him, nor hand of man bury him; let the darkness of the grave [or spirits] receive him."

But Cynvelin was their lord; he possessed his own lands and flocks from which he obtained his food; his slaves were numerous, and they were obliged to obey their master rather than the priest; so Leirwg had to form some other plan of revenge on Cynvelin than that of excommunication.

Leirwg was not long in settling in his own mind his course of action. A cruel smile played around his thin lips. He felt he could act in such a way that the fear of the gods would come back in that household. Hulda was still in his power. Venissa must be brought back and, through her, Alaric. Leirwg's shrewd eyes had long ago discovered that Alaric loved Venissa and, as Venissa would inherit her father's riches at his death, Leirwg was determined to fight hard for the recovery of his old power over these young people. And, if he failed !—Leirwg stood still a moment, a cunning expression showed in his eyes, as he thought: " Failing that, there is yet another way by means of which I can keep my hold on the riches of Cynvelin. I am pretty sure of Hulda."

Leirwg strode on to his house satisfied with his plans and determined to carry them out at all costs. At the gateway of his dwelling, he noticed a crawling beetle, and he stopped to crush it.

"So," he said to himself, "shall I crush all who oppose me and my religion."

On the evening of that same day, Leirwg visited Cynvelin's home. He was welcomed by Hulda who still gave him allegiance. She, Venissa and Julia were seated together. Venissa was teaching Julia to embroider with wool on a coarse piece of linen; the child was taking great pains, and Venissa praised her efforts while Hulda smilingly watched them both. It was a pretty domestic scene and might have softened a heart less hard than Leirwg's, but he knew no pity; although outwardly suave, inwardly he was full of cruel intentions.

Hulda bowed low before him and craved his blessing which he gave. Venissa stood upright and merely gave him a polite bow and said, "good evening," while Julia hid behind Venissa. Poor child, she still had a memory of the days spent in his charge, and dreaded to see the man appear.

"Don't let him have me, 'Nissa," she whispered.

"You need not be frightened, darling; you belong to me now," Venissa said softly, in reply, putting her arm around the little shrinking figure.

Hulda spoke sharply: "Julia, don't hide. Come and kneel before Leirwg, and he will give you his blessing."

Julia reluctantly obeyed, but Leirwg gave her scant notice.

"I would like to have a few words with you, Hulda," he said, and Hulda told Venissa to go with Julia into another room.

Immediately the two had departed with pleasurable haste, Leirwg spoke: "Hulda, I wish to know whether your husband and daughter are still determined to desert the worship of their ancestors' gods and follow this religion, the knowledge of which Bernard has brought to this place."

"Father, I—I—." Hulda hesitated, and flushed. Leirwg spoke harshly: "Hulda, do not dare to hide the truth from me. It will be in vain for, if you attempt such a thing, I shall find out for myself and punishment will fall on you as well as on your husband and daughter."

"I fear they are still obstinate," Hulda replied.

"And you, Hulda?"

"Oh, no, no. I dare not accept the teaching. I fear the wrath of the gods. I am utterly miserable, for I see my husband and Venissa are happy, and yet I dare not join them in their belief."

"Do not be foolish, Hulda. Happy indeed! They are mad, misguided, fooled by this Bernard. He has bewitched them, and it will end in disaster. The curse of the gods will fall upon them; they will sicken and die, or in some other way suffer. Your only safety is in listening to what I say and doing what I bid you. Now, I will be patient, and give you a chance to win back these two to the religion of their forefathers. You must use your womanly wit, and your power as a wife and mother, to persuade them to drop this nonsense."

"I will, I assure you; I will do my best; only do not let your curse be upon them. I will talk to my husband, and I will lay my commands upon Venissa; she has always been obedient to me."

"That is well. But if they are still obstinate, the gods will take vengeance. It is not a question of my curse, although, perhaps, I do have a certain amount of power, but I cannot hold back the curse of the gods that will fall upon them without doubt if they continue in this way of evil. And, while you are exerting your influence, it will be well if you can talk to young Alaric. Foolish, headstrong youth, the result of having always been allowed his own way is that now he has succumbed to this pernicious doctrine. His old father is terribly indifferent to religion and cares not what Alaric takes up, so long as the lad is happy. He dotes on his son, but I am inclined to think the old man is in his second childhood. Has it occurred to you, Hulda, that Alaric is in love with Venissa?"

"Yes, Leirwg, my husband and I both think so, but we are in no hurry to spare our daughter; she is only eighteen and simple and childlike in her outlook on life; we wish her to continue so as long as possible. I think she still only considers Alaric as a friend, as she has always done."

"Well, Hulda, you realise the importance of both Alaric and Venissa returning to the worship of our gods. They will be lord and lady here in years to come and, as such, important people; that is, if they listen to the wisdom of their elders, I mean you and myself; otherwise, I doubt if they will reach the prime of life; the gods will be avenged."

Hulda shuddered.

"Do not speak of the years to come when Cynvelin and I will be no more; I never think of death, if I can help it; it is so dark; so terrible. And, I pray you, do not threaten my child so. I hope she will have a happy, long life."

"You are weak and foolish, Hulda. Know this, that neither Cynvelin, Alaric nor Venissa can prosper without the favour of the gods, so everything in the future depends on whether you can win them back to the old ways. By the way, where is Bernard now, that hateful old disturber of the peace?"

"He is away on a preaching tour just at the present, Leirwg."

"It would be well if he never returned. Now, I must leave you; my time is precious, and I have much to attend to. Remember my commands; use all your skill and powers of persuasion to win back your people to our worship. I shall expect to hear good news from you before long."

So saying, the Arch-Druid took his departure.

Hulda at once sought her husband, determined to lose no time in her efforts to bring him back to his old devotion to the Druidical religion. She found him in an inner chamber and, as she paused in the doorway, she heard him repeating some words to himself, words that she recognised as having been taught him by Bernard. She remembered how Bernard had told them they were words the Lord Jesus had said to His disciples and had been written down by one of His followers, Matthew by name.

Hulda slowed her footsteps and listened.

"Blessed are the poor in spirit, for theirs is the Kingdom of Heaven."

Hulda stamped her foot impatiently.

"Poor in spirit, indeed!" How weak, how foolish the words sounded to her.

The stamp of her foot arrested Cynvelin's attention. He turned toward his wife with a smile of welcome, stopping in his recitation, having already repeated to himself the first four chapters of the Gospel according to St. Matthew. The early Britons had marvellous memories. It was considered a disgrace to be able to read and write, at any rate by the ordinary people. The Druids taught that it was a sacrilege to commit sacred matter to writing. Any legend, any bit of history told to them, they learnt by heart with the greatest of ease; they thought that only those who had poor memories needed have anything written on parchment. Education for a British gentleman consisted of music, painting, impromptu poetry, and athletic exercises. The women folk added to the music and painting, needlework, a little surgery, the mixing of medicines, weaving and spinning.

Now, when Bernard repeated or read to them the words of the Bible, those who desired to do so, learnt them without any trouble.

"Cynvelin, I wish to talk with you," Hulda said as she entered the room and sat down on a low stool which Cynvelin rose and offered her.

"I am always ready to listen to your voice, dear one," Cynvelin answered with a bright smile, but Hulda's face was grave.

"Oh, my husband," she continued, "let me beg of you to have done with these foolish ideas which Bernard has been teaching you. Leirwg has been here and he says the curse of the gods will be on you, if you persist in worshipping this new god."

"Hulda, these false gods have no power; they do not exist. The god that is supposed to dwell in the oak is a myth, an imagination of the priests. It is wrong to worship the sun or the moon. We should worship the Creator, not the thing created. I fear not the curse of the gods, for, as I said, they have no power."

"But, Cynvelin, even if it is as you say that the gods have no power, Leirwg has. I fear him more than the gods."

"Ah, my dear, you may be right there, although I doubt if he would dare to interfere with me; after all, I am the chief of our tribe, and I believe all my people would rise in my defence. And I remember how Bernard told me that Christ, my Saviour, said to Pilate, who condemned Him to death: 'Thou couldest have no power at all against me, except it were given thee from above.' So Leirwg cannot injure me, unless my Heavenly Father permits him to do so, and if it is His will that I should suffer for His sake as a witness to the truth, He will give me grace and strength to endure."

"Cynvelin, do not talk so lightly of suffering. Oh my husband, again I beg of you, for my sake, for Venissa's sake, come back to the service of our gods. Proclaim a special feast, make an offering, and so appease Leirwg's wrath, and save us all from sorrow."

Hulda flung herself on her knees beside her husband's chair and burst into tears.

Cynvelin was greatly moved. He rose and lifted her from the ground, putting his arms around her.

A strong temptation to yield to her pleading took possession of him for a few moments, but a voice of power and love, the voice of his Saviour, sounded in his heart: "If any man loves his father or mother more than Me, he is not worthy of Me." At that moment he realised that not even his wife must come between him and the One Who had redeemed him at such tremendous cost. With an upward look and an inward cry for help and grace, strength was given.

"My wife, my dearest on earth, I cannot deny my Saviour. I was lost, and He found me. He has pardoned my sins. He has filled my soul with love and peace. He has given me hope for eternity. I cannot relinquish Him, and He will not let me go. Hulda, my wife, I only long that you may share these blessings with me. Will you not seek the Lord Jesus yourself? Together, we will shake off the bondage of idol worship, together we will close our house to Leirwg and, in simplicity and truth, follow the Lord, seeking to win others for Him."

Cynvelin's pleadings were in vain. Hulda's only reply was: "Oh, Cynvelin, the wrath of the gods will fall upon you, upon us all. Why, why are you so stubborn? I do not understand what you say; there seems to me no sense in your remarks. Oh, Cynvelin, Cynvelin!"

Her voice rose to a wail of sorrow, and with a sob partly of pain, partly of anger, she left the room, and Cynvelin was alone once again.

He fell on his knees and prayed long and earnestly, first with his heart torn with suffering; then, as he sought help, peace came and with triumph he was able to say, "Lord, I only want Thy will for myself and my dear ones."

Chapter 12.

Leirwg's Commands.

NOT many days passed before Leirwg returned and demanded a private interview with Hulda. He asked how she had succeeded in her mission.

"I have failed utterly, Leirwg. My husband refuses to listen to my pleading. Truly, I think Bernard has bewitched him."

"Probably so, my daughter. I had thought of that, and to aid you in your good work of reclaiming your husband, I have brought you this."

. "In this bottle is a potion, and if you put a few drops in Cynvelin's food, it will counteract Bernard's baneful influence."

Hulda, as all women of her time, was well accustomed to the idea of administering some concoction to defeat an enemy's purpose; to ward off the ills of witchcraft; to win favour from some desirable quarter, or to win love, so she readily agreed to carry out Leirwg's instruction.

"Do not," the priest continued, "let the bottle out of your own keeping. Give the drops to Cynvelin only and that without his knowledge. Success depends on carrying out these directions with care."

"I will do exactly what you say. I would do anything to win my husband back to the old worship."

"That is well, Hulda. And Venissa, have you laid your commands on your daughter?"

"Not yet. She is young and happy. I do not wish to upset her or bring a shadow on her life."

"Nonsense! The shadows will fall sooner than you think, if things do not greatly change in this household, and if Venissa does not do as we wish. She will not escape any more than Cynvelin. Be sure of that."

Leirwg spoke haughtily, and Hulda was cowed. She said meekly: "I am sure Venissa will come back to the old worship when I insist and, Leirwg, what do you mean that Cynvelin will not escape? I thought you were sure that this potion would work wonders, that if I administer it secretly, his mind will change."

Leirwg made no reply; he seemed to be listening intently. Presently, he spoke: "What is that I hear?"

Going to the window, both of them looked into the courtyard and saw Venissa and Julia seated on the grass only a few yards away from the house. They were both singing, Julia's childish voice mingling with Venissa's sweet treble. The words could be heard clearly by the two listeners:

"Thou art the Guard of the babes that are playing.
Thou art the Guide of the souls that are straying.
Thou art the Helmsman that ruleth the deep.
Thou art the Shepherd that keepeth the sheep.

Gathered before Thee from every zone,
Lord, we seek shelter at foot of Thy throne:
Guileless and pure be our lips while we sing,
Thee, our Commander, 0h Christ! and our King.

Christ of the Father, the conquering Word!
Christ, the one Leader of saints of the Lord:
Wisdom, that sat on the throne of creation—
Patience, unswerving through all tribulation.

Born of a woman, a Babe in a manger,
Jesus our Saviour, our Pilot in danger:
Teacher and Husbandman, Lighthouse and Rock,
Pastor that yieldeth His life for the flock.

Fisher of men, by Gennesaret ever,
Casting the Gospel-net, wearying never;
Us, silly fish, from the ocean of sin,
Sweetly Thou callest, and gatherest in.

What can we add to Thy fullness of praise?
Worms of Thine earth-dust, Thy glory we raise!
Peace Thou hast purchased for souls dead before Thee—
Christ, we exalt Thy Name! God we adore Thee." [7]

Leirwg stood spellbound. It seemed as if even his hard heart was moved by the song and the beauty of the singers. Hulda was herself surprised that he stood so still and listened quietly until the song was finished. However, directly it ceased, he shook himself impatiently and asked: "Where did they learn that nonsense?"

---

[7] The oldest Christian hymn extant and the only one which dates back to the generation succeeding the apostles, the long hymn of Clement, now beginning to be revived among us by very free translations

"It is a hymn that Bernard taught them. I understand it was written by one Clement, and translated into our tongue from the Greek," Hulda explained.

"I will deal with Venissa some other time," Leirwg said. "And, as for that child Julia, better I had had my way and sacrificed her to the gods."

He turned away muttering to himself: "It may not be too late even now, with Cynvelin gone—" he broke off and glanced at Hulda; had she heard his words? But no, she was still looking out the window and her face, so lately clouded, was now smiling as she watched Venissa and Julia.

They had stopped singing, and Julia was tucking flowers into the golden headband that bound Venissa's hair. Both were laughing merrily and, for the moment, Hulda had forgotten her troubles, as she lingered at the window.

Leirwg gone, she joined her dear ones in the grounds. Venissa sprang up and brought a carved stool for her mother, while she and Julia sat at her feet. Hulda was silent wondering how best she could persuade Venissa to take notice of what she had to say. Julia was chattering happily about the flowers and the pet hens that came fearlessly around. The Britons kept hens for the sake of their eggs, and as pets; they never thought of eating them, and considered it a disgusting habit of the Romans to do so.

Presently, Julia said: "Venissa, haven't I got a proper name? You are Venissa ap Cynvelin, ap Maur, ap Lucius, ap Glvan, ap —; oh, I can't remember them all. But I am just Julia." "Yes, you are just my darling, little Julia. Isn't that enough, my pet?"

"Yes, but did I live here always? Sometimes, I think I remember another lady and a boy and —."

Venissa glanced at her mother, who said: "Julia dear, run away to Amelia. You can ask her to give you some bread and honey and go with her to the fields to gather elderberries; she is going to make some wine."

Julia ran off, forgetting her memories for the time being.

"Mother," Venissa asked, "shall we have to tell her who she is when she gets a little older, or at least what we know about her?"

"I don't know, child. I am thinking of more important things than that. Come with me into the house; I have something to say to you which I do not wish other ears to hear."

Venissa looked surprised and followed her mother into the house. No sooner were they seated than Hulda said: "Venissa, I cannot allow you to have further conversation with Bernard. He is a dangerous man and full of ideas about religion that we cannot accept. You must promise me now to forget all he has told you about this other god, and you must come with me to the next gathering in the sacred grove and do homage to our gods."

"But, mother, father has accepted Bernard's teaching."

"I know that, but I can tell you with confidence that your father will soon return to the worship of the gods which our forefathers reverenced."

"Oh, no, mother! It cannot be so. Has he told you that he will deny the Saviour Who died for him? Oh, mother, that would be terrible."

"Be quiet, child. Your father has not promised me this, but I have reasons for being confident that he will soon do as I say. However, I forbid you to mention what I say to him. I tell you as a secret. Now forget your father and think of yourself. Venissa, you have always obeyed me, and I expect you to be submissive now."

"Mother, I cannot accept these false gods any longer. Do not command me, I pray you, to worship them. In everything else I will seek to please you, but I cannot deny my Lord and Saviour."

"Enough, Venissa. I warn you Leirwg is not to be trifled with; you will suffer if you disobey my commands which are also his."

"Mother, is that not it? Leirwg must not be trifled with; we fear him more than we do the gods."

"Certainly not. Leirwg is only their representative, and although he may be persuaded to let you and your father escape punishment, the gods will not. In some way, their wrath will fall upon you. Oh, my child, do not be obstinate; I cannot bear to think of what will happen to you if you persist in this folly. Am I to be left desolate, a widow and childless, because of this departure from the religion of our forefathers?"

Hulda's voice had changed from one of command to one of entreaty, but before Venissa could reply, a curtain which hung over the door was drawn back and a young man, dressed in the blue garments of a slave, appeared. The young man carried a basin of water and had a towel thrown over his shoulder. His presence with the basin and towel meant that a meal was ready.

Hulda and Venissa, after washing their hands, went to the room where the mid-day meal was served. Cynvelin was there already, and Hulda and he seated themselves. Venissa, with an attendant, saw her father and mother served before she took her place at the table.

"Where is our little Julia?" Cynvelin asked, and Hulda answered:

"She has gone to the fields with Amelia. I thought it would be a treat for her; she had some bread and honey before she started."

"I miss her when she is absent," Cynvelin responded.

"Father, to-day Julia was asking about her name. She knows we all repeat our pedigree and she seems surprised that she has not been taught a genealogical recitation. Shall we have to tell her soon that she is not really ours?"

"Not yet, dear. Plenty of time for that later. It seems strange to me that there have never been any inquiries made concerning her. However, I am quite content that it is so. I should be sorry to part with our little sunbeam now."

Hulda was taking no part in the conversation; her mind was busy. The little phial which Leirwg had given lay in the folds of her gown, but she saw no opportunity of administering it to her husband at the moment; she was thinking as to how she could best manage it, and decided that she must wait for a more favourable chance. The responsibility of it made her feel and look grave, but when Cynvelin smilingly asked what was the reason of her silence, she replied that she was a little tired. Her husband was at once concerned and told her she must rest that afternoon; turning to Venissa, he said: "Venissa, see that no one disturbs your mother," which Venissa willingly promised to do.

Chapter 13.

Cynvelin Is Ill.

A few days later, Alaric was delighted to find Venissa alone when he visited Cynvelin's dwelling. Now that Venissa was no longer a child, Hulda was most particular that when Alaric or any young acquaintance of the opposite sex visited them, either she herself or a trusted attendant should be with her daughter; such was the etiquette of the times. However, at this time she was busy elsewhere and ignorant of the fact that Alaric had arrived.

"All alone, Venissa? I am fortunate today. It is long since I have been able to talk to you without a listener," Alaric said, as he entered.

Venissa smiled, but her eyes were sorrowful. Alaric was quick to notice it. "Is anything wrong, dear heart?" he asked.

"My father is ill. He was taken with sickness and great pain yesterday. He recovered towards evening, but today, after our mid-day meal, the trouble returned. My mother sent for Leirwg, for you know what a knowledge he has of medicine. He has given father a draught but the pain still persists. And, oh, Alaric! What do you think Leirwg says? It is the curse of the gods falling on my father, because he has forsaken the old worship."

"We know better than that, Venissa. We know they have no power. Do not let Leirwg shake your faith. But I am sorry your father is ill."

"My mother firmly believes what Leirwg tells her. How I wish Bernard were here; he would be a comfort to my father. If only his preaching tour had ended. Do you think he is likely to come soon?"

"Venissa, I wanted to tell you about Bernard. I have been trying to see you alone for days to tell you what I heard a short time ago in the forest. Quite unexpectedly, I came near the place where the priests were holding a meeting. They were so absorbed in their discussion that they did not notice my approach and, when I caught Bernard's name being mentioned, I took care to hide myself in a thicket. I found out that they are plotting to get rid of him, thinking that if he is gone, all of us who have learnt through him to love the Lord Jesus will soon return to the worship of the false gods."

"Alaric, do you think they would kill him?"

"I believe they would if they could get him. So, Venissa, as soon as he returns, we must warn him to go away from this neighbourhood."

"How we shall miss him! Who will teach us the words we love to hear and learn?"

"Christ Himself will be our Teacher, Venissa. I know we shall indeed miss Bernard, but we must not depend on him too much."

"I wish I had been more diligent in learning the words of Scripture, Alaric," Venissa said regretfully.

"Why, Venissa, you have been diligent. You can say many portions."

"Yes, but I might have learnt more. I can repeat the Gospel according to Mark, Paul's letter to the Romans, and I was learning the Gospel by John when Bernard left. Bernard says that John knew our

Lord in His earthly days. In some parts of our country the good news has been known for many years. We here in Devon have been ignorant, and if the Druids could have their way, we should remain ignorant."

"Well, now that we have received the good news, it is for us to hold it fast and spread it, Venissa. May God enable us to keep faithful."

Venissa was about to reply when she was interrupted by the entrance of her mother who exclaimed with astonishment: "You here, Alaric. You should have let me know, Venissa."

Hulda's voice was reproving, and Venissa flushed. She made no answer, and Hulda continued, turning to Alaric: "However, I am glad to see you, Alaric, for my husband has just bidden me send a messenger to your home to fetch you. Cynvelin wishes to have speech with you."

"How is he, mother?" Venissa asked eagerly.

"No better, my child; nor will he be until he renounces this new religion. Oh, Venissa, you and your father are breaking my heart. I curse the day when Bernard came into our midst. The happiness of my home is broken. Why are you so obstinate?"

"Mother, if only you would join us; if only you would accept Christ, we should be happy together."

For a moment, Hulda hesitated. She felt an inner urge, a longing which she herself could not have explained; then, suddenly, she seemed to see before her the strong face of the Druidical priest; she felt again the influence of his strange power and she shook herself free from the Spirit's pleading in her heart and answered: "You foolish child, don't you understand? It is I, and I alone, who stand between you and the wrath of the gods."

"Say rather the wrath of the priests," Alaric interposed.

Hulda turned on him angrily.

"Alaric, if you encourage Venissa in this foolishness and rashness, I shall forbid your coming to the house. But go now to my husband, and see for yourself what defying the gods has brought upon him.

Leirwg warned me it would be so, and, alas, alas, I fear the worst evil is yet to come!"

Hulda's voice broke in a sob, and Venissa put her arm around her mother, seeking to comfort her, while Alaric, feeling powerless to help, hastened to obey Hulda's command, and went to Cynvelin.

Alaric started in alarm, as he entered the bedroom, for Cynvelin looked terribly ill. His face was ashen, his eyes sunken as he lay back on a huge feather bed, but without pillows. [8] The sick man smiled as Alaric drew near to him, and was welcomed by the sick man.

"I am glad to see you, my lad. You have come quickly."

"I was here, sir, so there was no need to send a message. I am grieved to see you so ill," Alaric answered.

"I fear I am stricken for my death. For myself, I have no shrinking. What a marvellous change the knowledge of Christ and His salvation makes in a man's outlook. No fear; no dread; just a looking forward to His call. But I am anxious about my dear ones, especially Venissa, for my wife is entirely under the dreadful influence of Leirwg. I do not wish to speak evil of any, for our Master in His word has forbidden it, and Leirwg has been most kind to me in this illness, giving me draughts, chafing my numbed limbs, and promising to come again soon, but you know, Alaric, although he himself at times may do good things, yet his teaching is false and the gods he worships are myths. I fear Hulda will do anything Leirwg tells her, even to the giving up of our daughter to sacrifice."

"God forbid," Alaric exclaimed.

"Alaric, my lad, I have sent for you to ask you to do all in your power to protect Venissa."

"Sir," Alaric replied, "I would give my life to save her from harm, for I love her dearly. I have been waiting until we were both old enough to ask you to give her to me. I know I am not worthy of her, but I would always do my best for her in every way, I can assure you."

"This is good hearing, Alaric, my friend. I know of no one to whom I would so willingly give my daughter. I must see about the betrothal

---

[8]. 'Pillows were introduced later by the Saxons, they were not used by the British.'

as soon as I feel equal to the exertion. I would rather have this settled before I go hence to return no more."

"Oh, sir, do not say that. Surely you will recover. This illness has come on you so suddenly, it will as suddenly depart."

"Well, Alaric, I cannot say. I feel a strange sinking between the bouts of pain such as I have never experienced before. But I commend my dear child, Venissa, under God, to you. I should like to see you united in matrimony before I die, if possible. Is your father willing for this?"

"Yes, indeed. You know how indulgent my father is to me; he refuses me nothing, and in this case he loves Venissa for her own sake. I am not troubled about his consent, but will Venissa be willing?"

"Why! surely. She has always been so fond of you."

"That is just the trouble, sir. She has always looked on me as a brother, and I have been almost her only companion; if I wed her now, suppose later she should meet someone she likes better, what then?"

Cynvelin smiled.

"I think you will be able to trust her, Alaric."

Suddenly the sick man groaned. "Oh, the pains are coming on again. Call my wife, please."

Alaric hastily summoned Hulda, who banished him from the sick room, saying: "Go at once to Leirwg, ask him to come, he gave my husband ease yesterday."

Alaric went off and rather reluctantly sought Leirwg. When he was found, Alaric gave his message and was puzzled by the sinister expression that briefly passed over Leirwg's face.

"I will go to Cynvelin at once, but I fear I can do little for him. Take warning, young man, and observe for yourself the fate that falls upon those who deny the gods."

Leirwg gave Alaric no opportunity for a reply, but left him abruptly.

Chapter 14.

Osmond Begins To Doubt.

ALARIC lost no time in returning to Cynvelin's home, but to his surprise he was met at the gate by a servant who seemingly was posted there. The man spoke hurriedly. "Our lady says no one is to be admitted. Our lord is very ill, and Leirwg says he is to be kept quiet. I heard Leirwg tell our mistress that he wishes no intruders and whatever Leirwg commands will be done."

"Can I not have speech with the young mistress?" Alaric asked.

"No, sir. I fear not. I have orders to disturb no one with messages."

Alaric produced a coin and offered it to the man. His eyes gleamed greedily, for the possession of a coin meant much to a slave. Alaric said: "This is yours, if you can bring your young lady here."

However, the slave shook his head.

"I dare not, sir. Our lady is very short-tempered these days, and I know not how I might be punished if I did not heed her commands. Besides, Leirwg himself also gave me the order and to disobey him is to incur the wrath of the gods."

Alaric turned away, and went home. Late that evening he again found his way to Venissa's home. It was dark, but poor Alaric was too restless to go to bed. He stood outside the stockade in the shadow of a tree, when suddenly, he thought he heard his name whispered: "Alaric, is that you?"

Alaric responded loudly: "Yes, who wants me?"

"Hush!" came the whispered response. "Come away into the woods; I have somewhat to tell you."

Alaric obeyed, and in a short time stood in the dense darkness of the forest.

"Who is it?" he asked, for he could see no one. Then he felt a hand on his arm.

"It is I, Osmond."

"You, Osmond! I thought you were away in the Druidical college in Caer Isca (Exeter)."

"I have been at home two days. Leirwg sent for me, I do not know why, and yet, perhaps, I can guess. Tell me, Alaric, is my Uncle Cynvelin seriously ill ?"

"Yes, indeed, he is, and he thinks he will not recover."

"He will not, if Leirwg is allowed to doctor him," Osmond said in a whisper.

"Whatever do you mean?" Alaric said, speaking clearly.

"Oh, hush, hush! I am imperilling my life to speak like this, but I feel I must. I cannot bear to think of sorrow falling on my cousin Venissa and my poor uncle who is so good and kind, being —"

Osmond broke off, afraid to say what was in his mind.

"Do tell me what you mean, Osmond? What is it you know?"

"I know so little; after all, it is only a suspicion. It is this: two days ago when I arrived here, having been summoned by Leirwg, I went straight to him before even going to my mother. One of the priests told me I should find him in his chamber. So I went there fearlessly. You know, or perhaps you do not, that there is a small inner room opening out of Leirwg's chamber where he prepares physics and keeps draughts and pills, plasters and potions. I knocked on the outer door, and he called out: 'Come in.' As I entered, he came out of this inner room and I smelt what I know to be a strong poison. I have helped Leirwg so many times in his work, distilling herbs and all that sort of thing, that I am quick to detect the different concoctions by their smell. I felt suspicious, and I think he noticed my look. I am told I betray myself by my expression often; anyhow, he said: 'Old Rover's days are numbered; he is deaf and blind; it is cruel to let him linger.' But I am told his old hound died a week ago, so Leirwg did not show his usual astuteness in that speech."

"Osmond, you can't think Leirwg is administering poison to Cynvelin? If that is so, how can we stop him? It is too terrible to contemplate."

"Remember, I have told you nothing definite, Alaric. I only wish to warn you to get into Cynvelin's chamber and stay there. Get Cynvelin to say you must nurse him and you may yet save him. Throw all medicines away and watch his food."

Alaric groaned.

"How can I? Hulda may refuse me entrance. And I should have no control over his food."

"Well, do your best."

"How can you have anything to do with such a horrible religion, Osmond? It is cruel and wicked."

Osmond sighed.

"Alaric, I am beginning to hate it. I am learning the ghastly methods and the hateful mysteries at my college. It is more false than you know, and my mother begs me to let her teach me of this Saviour of Whom Bernard has taught her. You scarcely know how full of deceit this religion is; just let me tell you of one instance. It may sound a trifling matter to you, but it is typical of all. Our priests say that the mistletoe is a sacred growth, planted in the oaks by the gods, untouched by the hand of man, and, when it is found growing on any tree, that tree is sacred and must be worshipped. A few months ago, I was sitting in solitude in a wood near Caer Isca (Exeter), thinking deeply, when I saw one of our priests approaching. I had no desire for human companionship at the moment, and I kept quiet, hidden by the dense undergrowth around me. I saw that the man was carrying a bundle of mistletoe twigs, the cut ends of which were enfolded in moist earth. I watched him climb a giant oak and with his bronze dagger make cuts in the bark, and in each slit he grafted a mistletoe twig, plastering the place with wet clay. My eyes were opened. The mistletoe, which I had been taught was a gift of the gods, was in actuality grown in the same manner as any other fruit-bearing plant."

Alaric laughed, and was about to remark that he was not sorry Osmond's faith in the Druids was being shaken, but before he could speak Osmond said: "What was that? Hush, listen!"

It was only some furry, four-footed inhabitant of the wood prowling through a thicket, but Osmond was scared and fled.

Alaric followed him more slowly, wondering what he had better do. His first impulse was to accuse Leirwg to his face, but, after consideration, he thought that would only aggravate the terrible old man to worse deeds of revenge, and what to do, Alaric could not decide.

He spent the night pacing around Cynvelin's grounds, but the stockade, which surrounded the dwelling, the outhouses, the slaves' quarters and the pleasure garden, was so high, the doors so barred, that Alaric was unable to find an entrance.

He could only wait for the morning.

Chapter 15.

Leirwg's Revenge.

"OH, my father! My father! What shall I do without him?"

The words in tones of bitter grief reached Alaric's ear as he entered Cynvelin's dwelling in the early morning. To his surprise, the slaves who unfastened the gate made no demur at his entrance. He was prepared to battle for it, but found there was no need to do so; he went in unchallenged.

Directly the sad words fell upon his ear he realised that Venissa was mourning for her father and, without ceremony, he entered the room where she was. "Venissa," he cried, "am I too late?"

Venissa held out her hands to him with the gesture of a trusting child. Her eyes were swollen with weeping, and she had difficulty in checking her tears and controlling her voice as she said: "He is gone, Alaric. My father whom I loved so dearly and who was my protector and guide."

"Then, alas, I am too late!" Alaric said, and Venissa asked: "What do you mean? Too late for what?"

"I came hoping to be in time to stop your father taking any more of Leirwg's medicine."

Again Venissa asked: "What do you mean?"

"It is useless to explain, Venissa, dear. I am too late."

A sudden illumination came to Venissa's mind. A hint was enough for her.

"Alaric! I know what you mean. Oh, that wicked, wicked man! But why should he wish to get rid of my father who never did him any harm?"

"I can think of more reasons than one, Venissa. But the principal reason, doubtless, was that your father had forsaken the old religion and was no longer a source of income to Leirwg. Cynvelin died for the truth; had he yielded to Hulda's pleadings and Leirwg's arguments and commands, he would be with us today. His was a martyr's death as truly as those who have suffered in Rome and other places, of whom Bernard has told us, and his will be the martyr's reward and crown. Tell me, dear, unless it hurts you too much to speak of it, did he suffer greatly?"

"Terribly. He said it felt as though his inside was burning; his face was grey and drawn. Leirwg," Venissa shuddered as she spoke the name, "was here all the early part of the night, pretending to help him with draughts, but towards morning the pain ceased and father said: 'I have no fear. I am going to be with my Saviour; He holds my hand.' His face grew calm and almost bright, and now he looks so peaceful. But, Alaric, what am I going to do without him? I am frightened, I have no one to protect me now, and I am terrified of what Leirwg may do."

"Venissa, dear heart, you have me. Your father put you into my care, and asked me to guard and defend you. You know, dear, it will be my greatest joy to cherish and care for you, keeping you from all ills, if it is in my power to so do."

Alaric put his arm around the girl and she clung to him saying: "You have always been a dear, big brother to me, and you always will be, I am sure."

Alaric winced, but he realised it was not the time to tell Venissa of his longing to be something more than a brother to her.

Presently, the two went together to look at all that was visible to the human eye of the loving parent. Two slaves stood motionless at the head of the couch and not by any movement or change of countenance did they show that they were conscious of Venissa's and Alaric's entrance.

Alaric was struck with the calm expression on Cynvelin's face; it almost looked like the dawning of a smile.

"He looks happy," Venissa whispered. "But, Alaric, death is like a door slammed in one's face; the one we love has gone through and we are left here in the cold."

"We shall go to him some day, dear heart, and we must not forget that the Saviour to Whom he has gone is with us. He will protect you even if I should be unable to do so. He has all power and will not fail the soul that trusts in Him."

Venissa lifted her bowed head.

"Alaric, I was forgetting. I could only think of my loss, but I do know that Jesus is with me; my father reminded me of that only yesterday, how His word says: 'I will never leave thee nor forsake thee.' "

"Come, dear, into the dining-hall, and let me persuade you to have some food. You look as though you had taken nothing for hours, perhaps days."

Venissa allowed Alaric to lead her, as though she were a little child, into another apartment. Here Alaric brought her fruit and bread, persuading her to eat a little.

"Where is the little one?" Alaric asked. And Venissa told him: "My mother sent her to my aunt's yesterday. I wondered at it then, as I did not think my father was going to die, but I am glad now, as I should not like Julia to know anything about death yet; she is too young. What shall I tell her when she returns?"

"Just tell her that Cynvelin has gone to live with Jesus, and is so happy, and that one day we shall go too."

As they were talking, Hulda, accompanied by Leirwg, came into the room.

Alaric could not help noticing how greatly Hulda had changed in the last few weeks. Her face, formerly so serene, was now drawn, white and haggard, while her eyes held a haunted, terror-stricken expression. Leirwg was as usual cold and stern.

Alaric and Venissa both arose at the entrance of their elders, and waited in silence. Hulda was about to speak but Leirwg checked her. "My daughter, I desire speech with these young people, especially Venissa. My child, did I not warn you that if your poor father persisted in his defiance of our gods, calamity would befall him? And as I said, so has it come to pass. Alas, the punishment has been more severe than even I anticipated! I did my best to ward off the blow but I failed for, although I am a priest, although I know many of the secrets of the gods, yet even I am powerless to avert their anger when one is so defiant and obstinate as Cynvelin was. Now, it is too late to save your father, Venissa; yet, it is not too late for you. Repent, return to the religion of your forefathers, make a special offering to the gods to induce them to receive you back into favour, and all will yet be well. You are young and, consequently, not as responsible as others. I am willing to pardon your wanderings and will guide you in the future, now that you have no father to do so."

Alaric's eyes flashed. Well he realised what Leirwg's promise of guidance meant. Leirwg's intention was to take control of the wealth that would now fall to Hulda and her daughter. Alaric chafed at the hypocrisy of the man, pretending that he had done his best to help Cynvelin, while all the time if it had not been for the priest's wickedness, Cynvelin would have been alive and well. It was with difficulty the lad kept quiet.

Leirwg waited for Venissa to speak, and hoped that in her sorrow she would be submissive, but he was disappointed.

Calmly the girl answered. “Sir, I cannot return to the old religion. Light has shone into my heart, and I cannot go back to the dark.”

“Light! What do you mean? Do you infer that I and your forefathers, your mother, and many of your friends, are in the dark?”

“Bernard told us some words spoken by our Saviour, God’s Son, Who came from Heaven to save us; He said: ‘This is the condemnation that Light is come into the world and men love darkness rather than light, because their deeds are evil.’ Jesus came as the Light of the world.”

Leirwg’s face was livid with rage. The simply spoken word had pierced him like an arrow. “Their deeds are evil!” He lifted his hand as though he would strike Venissa, but Alaric stepped in front of her, asking boldly: “Sir, is not that so? Can you say there has been no evil deed done in this house recently?”

There was stillness in the room for a moment. Hulda hid her face in terror, Venissa grew white as she wondered what would be Leirwg’s response to such outspokenness. It looked as if Leirwg was about to lose his usual calm; however, the habit of years triumphed, he kept control of himself, but spoke bitterly: “You young fools. There is only one thing in your favour, and that is your youth. One must always allow for a certain amount of folly in young people, but I warn you, although I am willing to wait patiently and give you time to repent of your silly, headstrong ways, there is a limit to my clemency, and I shall take steps to bring you to your senses. What is more, although I may wait, it is possible the gods will not be so merciful as I, and judgement may fall from them upon you both. If they act, even I cannot save you. You have seen that for yourselves in this case.”

“Venissa, Venissa, my child,” Hulda cried, holding out her hands in entreaty, “I beseech you, be persuaded; give up this terrible thing which has caused your father’s death. He would be with us today in health and strength, had he not defied the gods who have now taken vengeance upon him. Do not break my heart, you are all I have left.” Hulda’s voice broke. Sobs shook her frame.

Venissa flung herself on her knees and put her young, strong arms around her mother, while Alaric said: “Lady, fear not the gods; they are but myths; they cannot harm you. Bernard told us some words from the Holy Writings, which said: 'They cannot do good, neither is it in them to do evil.' "

"Dearest," Venissa added, "won't you join us in worshipping the one true God? He will bring comfort to your sorrowing heart. Father is with God, and we shall go to him, if we trust the Saviour Who died on the Cross for us. Bernard will teach you when he returns, if you will listen to him."

"Bernard, Bernard!" The priest muttered. "Nothing but the name of that wretched man.

Leirwg was persuading himself that he was acting in zeal for the gods in all that he did, and was blind to the fact that fierce jealousy of Bernard had a great deal to do with his anger at the defection of his former followers.

Aloud he said: "Bernard has left the neighbourhood, and I think it is doubtful if he will ever return. The gods have probably dealt with him as he deserves. It is of no use for you to lean on him. Remember, Venissa, I am now your guardian, and it is to me you will yield obedience as in former days you did to your father Cynvelin. We will say no more now," he added, seeing how unfit Venissa looked for discussion at the moment.

"I must not stay with you longer," he continued. "I have neglected many duties in order to be in this house of sorrow; I must now attend to them."

Then, turning to Alaric, he said sternly: "Take care, young man, how you encourage Venissa in rebellion. You may repent too late when you see the wrath of the gods falling on her, as it will do, unless she is dutiful to me and her mother. Moreover, I shall take steps to prevent you visiting here, if you continue in your mistaken views."

As Leirwg left the room, he said to Hulda: "Leave everything in my hands, my daughter. You wish to make a special sacrifice to appease, if possible, the gods?"

"Yes, yes indeed. Anything to protect my child and myself."

"The only safe path for your daughter lies in complete, wholehearted return to the religion of her forefathers; it is useless to pretend anything else, Hulda. You must see to it that she obeys my commands. I look to you for this; otherwise, I shall be powerless to save her from her fate.

So saying, Leirwg departed, leaving a broken-hearted woman and a stricken girl behind him.

Chapter 16.

Elfrida

OSMOND stood with meekly folded hands listening to his superior. Leirwg had been talking at some length; now he summed up all he had been saying in a few terse sentences.

"You understand, Osmond, what I mean. It is not often that I take a subordinate into my confidence. I am trusting you and I think you will not prove an unworthy disciple."

Leirwg paused, his dark, piercing eyes seeming to Osmond to penetrate to his innermost being and it needed all the young priest's control to prevent himself shifting uneasily. He knew if he gave any evidence of anxiety, Leirwg would distrust his loyalty, and Osmond was still under the older man's spell, still in bondage to the superstitions which had held his ancestors in the grip of fear and which had been passed on to him and his fellows.

Leirwg waited in silence. Osmond at last replied: "Sir, I understand what you require, and will hasten to do your bidding."

"That is well, but in order that there shall be no mistake, state what you are to do."

"I am to return home and say farewell to my mother, leading her to conclude that I am about to return to my college in Caer Isca. Then, I am to return here, put on the disguise you will have ready for me and go forth, seeking to discover the whereabouts of Bernard. I am to appear to him as an inquirer into this new religion, and, when I have gained his confidence and learnt his movements, I am to send a messenger to you letting you know where he is and where he is likely to be going."

"Well said, my son. That is your task. Then, I shall dispatch trusted servants to the spot, and we shall have no further trouble with this pestilent man. It is a good thing that Bernard does not know you. You tell me that although you have watched him at times, yet you have never made yourself conspicuous or drawn attention to yourself in any way."

"That is so, sir," Osmond replied.

"Now go and spend an hour with your mother. I shall expect you back at dusk. It will be well for you to make a start in the dark."

Leirwg suddenly frowned, and Osmond wondered, for he did not guess that Venissa's words came to Leirwg's memory at that moment.

"Men love darkness rather than light because their deeds are evil."

"Words, mere words," Leirwg muttered. "Why should the words of a slip of a girl haunt me?"

Ah! Leirwg knew not that the words were not Venissa's but the words of the Lord of Life, the Son of God, Whom Leirwg was defying and working against, in league with the enemy of souls.

Osmond, leaving his master, hastened to his mother's home. His face was gloomy, for he hated the task that lay in front of him. Naturally of an open, frank disposition, it was not easy for him to adopt the underhanded methods his instructors wished and which they themselves practised daily.

His mother, Elfrida, was seated under a veranda, some needlework lay on her lap, but just then her hands were idle, her eyes were uplifted to the sky, and a soft murmur of song reached Osmond's ear as he drew near. Elfrida was singing some verses of the same hymn that Venissa and Julia had sung on the day when Leirwg listened with great annoyance.

Osmond paused, keeping out of sight, as he listened to his mother. The words reached him clearly:

"Born of a woman, a babe in a manger,
Jesus our Saviour, our Pilot in danger;
Teacher and Husbandman, Lighthouse and Rock,
Pastor that yieldeth His life for the flock.

What can we add to Thy fullness of praise?
Worms of Thine earth-dust, Thy glory we raise!
Peace Thou hast purchased for souls dead before Thee;
Christ we exalt Thy Name! God we adore Thee."

Osmond's heart was greatly stirred as he watched and listened. His mother's face was radiant, the face which Osmond had so long known as sorrowful and care-worn was now completely changed, lit with joy and shining with peace. The words of the song were so utterly different from any of the national odes or old rhymes to which Osmond had been accustomed all his life.

"Peace! Glory! Praise! One that yieldeth His life for the flock!" What remarkable words! It was inexplicable. The young man felt he could not understand what had taken place to so transfigure his mother and put such a song into her mouth.

He stepped forward into Elfrida's line of vision. She gave a little exclamation of joy and welcome, and Osmond seated himself beside her.

"You look worn, my son. Have you been spending nights in vigil at Leirwg's bidding?"

"No, mother. I have had good sleep; at least, I should have done so, if my thoughts had not been so busy at times. It is perhaps just as well that I am to return to my college at once and resume my studies at Caer Isca."

Osmond felt ashamed of himself as he deliberately made this statement and deceived his mother. He hated the commands that made it necessary for him to lie.

"Oh, my son, I am sorry your holiday is over! How I wish you were never returning to your college. Osmond, had I known years ago what I now know, I would never have consented to Leirwg's suggestion that you should become a priest. Osmond, is it too late? Can you not break loose from it all? I need you here. I am growing older. I am not so strong as I was, and there is need of a man's head and hand to guide and control our many servants. Besides, more important than that, I have learnt to hate the false worship to which you are devoting your life, and I would rather set you free from its bondage."

"Mother, it is unthinkable. Why! my life would not be worth a straw. Once started on a priest's life, it is binding for all time. I have learnt some of the Druidical secrets. I am being initiated into their ceremonies. You must remember, mother, our Druidical priests only entrust their wisdom to those who they suppose will keep them secret; that is why their knowledge is never written down but only passed on by word of mouth and kept in the memory of those who are instructed in the religion. I am sworn to loyalty. I should most certainly be put to death, if I broke away. No, alas! I am as one caught in a trap ; there is no escape."

"Oh, Osmond, my dearest. I would you knew the Saviour Who has brought such joy into my heart, then you would be willing to risk even life itself to serve Him. Listen, Osmond," Elfrida continued, as Osmond was about to speak, "I have been thinking today of what one of our bards told us some years ago. He said an ancient chief was seated in his hut one evening, surrounded by his followers, when a little bird flew in through an opening in the wall; it fluttered across the room and then found its way out through another opening. 'Ah,' said this wise old chief, 'is that not like us? We come from the dark, we flutter awhile in the light, then we go into the dark again and are soon forgotten; we go, we know not whither.' Osmond, my son, that is a picture of human life without the Saviour; that is the life I have known in the past, but now I know that when this short, uncertain life is over I shall go into the Light of the love of God."

"Mother! How can you know? How can a few words spoken to you by Bernard have brought this change to you? Your transformed attitude passes my understanding, mother. Bernard must possess singular power."

"My son, it is the power of the Holy Spirit. He has taught me. Let me try to explain. I lived in fear; even when I was a young girl I was always thinking what more could I do to be acceptable to the gods. I would sacrifice anything to win their favour and was naturally of a timid disposition, so many things terrified me: the darkness as it fell night by night, the howling of the wind, thunder and lightning, when it came; the thought of evil spirits; the gods themselves, and, most of all, death. Death that must come to all. The priests told me that if I sacrificed that which was most precious to me, the gods would favour me in the spirit world. I could not understand them but I obeyed. I gave my Ida, my lovely child, not for my own sake then, but because her father, my dear husband, had just departed this life, and it was to help him, I made the offering. They told me, too, it was better for the little one; it would mean happiness for her. My heart was torn, but I listened to them and did what they suggested. I sent you away that you might not know about it; you were then ten years old, and I did not want your young life clouded. Then, I gave of my wealth to Leirwg and, finally, I gave you, my son, to be a priest. But no sacrifice brought peace. When Bernard came, he told us of a God of Love, of a Saviour Whose sacrifice atoned for our sins. Osmond, it was like healing ointment on my wounded heart; it brought rest to my weary soul from the first moment I heard the story. Directly I heard of the Saviour, I began to long for a deeper knowledge of Him. I asked Him to reveal Himself to me and He has done so; to me, just a poor, weak, sinful woman. He has given me rest, I know not how, and peace to which I had always been a stranger."

Elfrida paused, and Osmond sighed.

"Something has certainly changed you, mother dear. I cannot but see that, and I see this alteration in others too; in Alaric, for one. He has become unselfish, considerate of others, even the slaves. I could almost wish," Osmond broke off. Then, after a pause, he continued: "Ah me, it is useless for me! I am bound hand and foot. I must continue in the religion of my ancestors. Leirwg prophesies great things for me. Mother, would you not be proud to see your son elected as Arch-Druid in years to come?"

"My boy, I would rather see you a slave, if you were a child of God. Osmond, what will earthly honours avail you in the day of death? I pray daily that you may be brought into the Light; that Christ may reveal to you that you are a sinner, and, then, that He is a Saviour."

"Mother! You forget that I am a priest. Why call me a sinner?"

"Osmond, think, my son, have you never sinned?"

Osmond flushed. He recalled the lie he had so recently told his mother, and many others before that. He was silent, and Elfrida continued: "I wish you were staying here longer, for when Bernard returns, I should ask him to teach you the wonderful story he has taught me."

Osmond tried to answer lightly.

"By the way, Bernard has apparently left this neighbourhood for good. Do you know where he has gone, mother?"

All unsuspecting that Osmond had any other motive than a passing interest in the matter, Elfrida replied: "It was his intention to go into Gwlad-yr-hav (Somerset) to preach the Gospel there, but he will return to us here, for he has many converts and he wishes to teach us more of the truth and nourish us in the faith."

Osmond rose abruptly.

"Well, I must be off, mother. Leirwg is expecting me to return to him before I start on my journey."

"But, Osmond, surely you will spend the night here. You cannot travel until daylight."

"Leirwg's orders are that I am to return to him as soon as I have bid you farewell, mother," Osmond answered evasively.

Elfrida sighed. She realised, as she had done many times previously, that her wishes counted for nothing as compared to the Arch-priest's orders.

"At least, you will have a meal before you go, dear," she said gently, and Osmond, remembering that he was to journey forth into the night and that it might be long hours before he would get the chance of another meal, readily consented.

Elfrida clapped her hands, and immediately a servant appeared to take her orders. Quite soon she and her son were seated before a well-spread board. Being the winter season, there was no fresh meat; most of the cattle, except those kept for breeding, were killed at the end of the summer, because of the difficulty of finding food for them in the cold season. The flesh was then dried and smoked for winter consumption. So now appeared dishes of the cured meat, fresh-water fish, honey, oatcakes, nuts, and rich cheese made from goat's milk. Osmond made a hearty meal, and then rose to go. He lingered a minute or two as though unwilling to leave. Generally he had left his home light-heartedly, but now he felt a great longing to remain with his mother. He hated the task allotted to him, and felt an impulse surging within him to defy Leirwg, to cast off the bonds that bound him, and declare he would no longer continue his apprenticeship; give up all thought of becoming a Druidical priest, and instead take up the home duties of farm and field, seeking to be a comfort to his mother in her old age. She looked frail, and her eyes were moist as she put her arms around him saying, "Must you go, my son?"

Osmond dare not tell her of the inner urge he felt. At that moment of weakness, he was afraid to listen to her pleading, so he said gruffly, seeking to hide his emotion: "You know, mother, I am bound to obey Leirwg. To break with him now would mean certain death. No man may enter the Druidical universities, begin to be initiated into the secrets and mysteries of their religion and then draw back. I should be slain without a doubt."

"Better to lose life itself, my son, than your soul," Elfrida answered, and Osmond gasped.

"Mother mine, you are indeed a changed woman; you who have always been so afraid of the death of the body for yourself and those whom you love, and now you can speak thus."

"Yes, dear, I know I am changed, for my Saviour is one Who can change hearts, taking away the fear that hath torment and giving us the courage of faith. I shall go on praying for you, my own dear son." Osmond's heart was too full for speech. He gave his mother a hearty embrace, and turned away without another word to go forth on the errand he loathed—to track down and betray to death the one who had been the means of bringing light and joy to his mother's heart.

Chapter 17.

The Plans Of Placidia.

PLACIDIA, wife of Felicius the Roman centurion, reclined in her dressing-room while her slave girls attended to her make-up. She had just returned from the baths where she had been massaged, anointed, perfumed, and now the minute details necessary to a Roman lady's idea of adornment were being carried out with elaborate care. One slave held a bronze mirror in front of her lady, while another arranged the lady's hair after having oiled, combed, and curled it. A low table, with carved legs, near at hand was strewn with hair-wash, perfumes, sweet-smelling creams, all contained in metal pots; on the table were also ivory combs, tweezers for plucking eyebrows, and boxes of rouge for tinting my lady's face. Canace, Placidia's daughter, was seated in the room; she held a wax tablet in her hand, and with a metal stylus was writing, at her mother's dictation, a list of articles which Placidia said must be obtained before they left Rome for their country seat.

Little Flora, now seven years old, came running into the room and asked what Canace was doing. When she heard, she clapped her hands with joy.

"Are we really going to the country soon? I am glad," the child said.

"I hope so, Flora, if your father consents. I am weary of the noise of the city. I am told that Rome is the noisiest city in the world, and I can well believe it."

"But, mother," Canace said, "it might be worse if wheeled traffic were allowed all day. Don't you think it is a good thing it is prohibited between the hours of sunrise and four o'clock?"

"Of course, child, I can hardly imagine what it would be like, if during the hot hours we had a continuous rattle of wheels over the cobble stones. But then, the larger part of the day comes after four, for I never retire to rest until twelve or even later."

"Anyhow, it will be lovely to go to the country," continued little Flora. "I remember last year, the peacocks and the flamingo, the geese, too. Canace, you remember them, don't you? And when we went to see the pigs fed, how funny they were; and father and Marcus took us fishing."

Flora was a chatterbox, and would have gone on talking whether her friends listened or not, if her mother had not checked her.

"Hush, child. I am not sure that you will be going."

Canace and Flora both exclaimed in dismay: "Mother, why not?"

"I cannot tell you now. It will depend on what your father says. Go now to your nurse. Flora and Canace, it is time for your lessons. Do not forget, both of you, to make your offering to the spirits of the dead as you pass through the atrium."

"Mother, you know I do not —" Canace began. Her mother interrupted her: "Do as you are bid, Canace, and don't argue. How many times have I told you that those spirits are kindly gods that protect children from the spectres and are pleased with a slight offering from the simple, pure spirit of a child?"

Canace and Flora left their mother's room, Canace looking grave and Flora in tears.

"Why am I not to go to the country, Canace?" the little one asked. "I love it. Nurse says I can run wild when we are there. I want to see the dormouse again."

"Perhaps you will go, darling. Don't fret," Canace said soothingly, but she had some misgivings on the subject, for she knew a little of the idea in her mother's mind.

Later in the day, Canace was again seated in her mother's room. Placidia, although full of faults, was yet a fond mother, and liked to have her children with her when convenient. Canace was pondering on the words which Placidia had spoken that morning to Flora.

She was wondering if she might ask for an explanation when Placidia herself brought up the subject.

"Canace, I must explain to you my plan for Flora, because the child is greatly influenced by your opinion and you can impress her with the honour and glory of the life which I hope may be hers."

Canace's big dark eyes were fixed on her mother as she listened.

"Don't stare at me like that, child. You look reproachful, and I want you to understand that I am seeking for your little sister the most honourable, exalted position possible. Yes, indeed, above that even of an empress. You have heard about the Vestal Virgins and, of course, you have seen them and been to the temple to watch them, but I doubt if you realise just what is the significance of their dedication. Vesta, the hearth goddess, is of great importance to all women and children; being a household divinity, you know, she is honoured in every home from the meanest hut to the most splendid palace, and in the temple a fire must be kept burning night and day in her honour; it must never go out; so six virgins are set apart to live in the temple and tend the fire. They are given over from their parents' control to that of the Pontifex Maximus, who is the head of the college of the priests."

"Oh, mother!" Canace interrupted, as she realised the meaning of her mother's words and thought of her happy, carefree, little sister condemned to such a life.

"Hush, I have not finished! There is now a vacancy in the sisterhood, one having reached the age of forty, at which time their period of service ends, and they are free to take up secular life and marry, if they should so wish. Any parent who possesses a girl-child between the age of six and ten, perfect in health and beauty, and of patrician birth, may enter her child's name as a candidate. I am desirous of doing this, and entering Flora, for it is a great honour to be the mother of a Vestal Virgin."

"But, mother, will Flora like it?"

"Not just at first, perhaps, but as she grows older her spirit will catch the fire of devotion and she will realise her exalted position. Why, Canace, a Vestal Virgin enjoys many privileges. When she goes out in her chariot, an officer precedes her bearing the insignia of authority, as is borne before the principal magistrate, and all passers-by salute her with great respect. The best place is reserved for her at the amphitheatre, and she has the casting vote as to whether a wounded gladiator is to be allowed to live or be killed. Just imagine our little Flora, when she is older, with every eye fixed on her in her white robes and white head-dress, and all awaiting her decision and bowing to her decree. Then, if she should meet a criminal in the street, on his way to death, she has the power to pardon and release him. Now, do you not think the position is worth coveting for Flora? You are just over the age, or I should have chosen you, for I think you are even more beautiful than your sister."

Canace shuddered.

"Mother, Flora would be happier on our farm, picking the flowers and feeding the birds, and I could not feed the fire in honour of a goddess, for father and Marcus have taught me to love Jesus, the Son of God."

"Canace, I forbid you talking like this. Woe is me! Why am I such an unfortunate woman? I have lost my baby Julia; my husband, my son, and now my daughter are forsaking the religion of their ancestors and taking up this new religion which seems to be chiefly the solace of the poor, the slaves, the despised. Canace, I shall be extremely angry with you, and shall punish you severely if you influence Flora against my wishes. I want her to go willingly and happily to her new life, if she is fortunate to be selected. The duties are not arduous; until she is twenty she will be learning her work and responsibilities. Then, for ten years, she will actually carry out her duties, keeping the sacred fire alight, pouring in oil and wine; cleansing the temple with water brought from the hallowed fountain of Egeria, and reciting prayers for the welfare of the city. Finally, from thirty to forty, she will teach others to fill her position when she leaves. Ah! here comes your father. I must get his consent without delay, as the time for the election is drawing near."

Felicius entered, followed by a slave carrying a large wicker tray.

"I have been to the Forum, and have brought you a little offering, dearest," Felicius said, smiling at his wife.

Placidia looked too bored to return her husband's smile, and he continued: "The children, too, I have not forgotten."

Placidia took the carved spoon which her husband presented to her, and remarked: "It is beautifully engraved; what have you brought the children?" [9]

Felicius lifted from the tray a basket which he handed to Canace. It was filled with small cakes made from honey and figs.

"The basket was made in Britain, Canace, and here is a present for Flora which I think she will like."

Placidia gave a scream as Felicius took from the tray a small cage wherein two white mice sported themselves.

Canace thanked her father, her eyes speaking more eloquently than her lips. She adored her father, and any gift from him was treasured, not only for its value, but because it was a token of his love.

---

[9] 'Roman fathers were noted for their habit of bringing home gifts to their children. Often friends presented men with little presents to carry to the young people.

"Where is Flora?" Felicius asked and, turning to the slave, he was about to bid the man summon the child when Placidia checked him.

"Do not send for Flora. I want to talk to you about her. Canace can stay; I have already explained to her what I propose for Flora."

"You can go," she continued, speaking to the slave, who quietly retired.

Felicius seated himself on the ivory couch and prepared to listen with toleration. But Placidia had only to make her opening remark in order to arouse his concern.

"You know, Felicius, there is a vacancy among the Vestal Virgins; the choice of a new one is to take place shortly, and I propose that we enter Flora's name as a candidate."

Felicius did not hesitate a moment.

"Most certainly not, Placidia. I would not entertain the idea for a second. My little Flora worshipping a heathen goddess! Horrible! I covet for her a life given to my Lord and Saviour, Jesus Christ, and spent for Him. Put it out of your mind immediately, my dear."

Placidia flushed angrily and began to remonstrate, but Felicius, knowing his wife could easily be turned from some plan of hers if something else engrossed her attention, said quickly: "I have some news for you which I hope will give you pleasure. I believe I am about to be ordered to Britain. Then we can resume our search for our darling little Julia. I fear the messengers I have sent on that errand have not been as thorough in their quest as we could have wished, but now we can execute it ourselves. Does it not please you, dearest?"

"Yes and no," Placidia answered. "I hate leaving Rome and all my friends for that barbarous country, but I do long for my child."

"Not barbarous now, Placidia. Britain is becoming highly civilised under Roman rule."

"Well, one thing I am glad of anyhow, that is that you will be away from the dreadful influence of those wretched Christians who gather in the catacombs. Perhaps there will be some hope of your returning to the religion of our land."

Felicius smiled.

"I shall still be under the control of my Master, and I hope by His grace to be able to spread the tidings of His love among the British."

Placidia lay back and closed her eyes while Canace crept close to her father and whispered: "Oh, father, I am glad you will not let Flora be a Vestal Virgin. I think she is beginning to love Jesus as we do, and I am afraid she would forget Him if we sent her away."

Felicius put his hand on the child's head with a loving gesture: "God bless you, my daughter," he said.

Chapter 18.

A Changed Man

OSMOND, as he tramped along in the darkness, was the subject of great conflict. His condition of mind was a puzzle even to himself.

"I feel," he thought, "as if I were two persons, one pulling in one direction, one in another."

He was far from realising that two were fighting for his soul. The Holy Spirit, of Whom Osmond had never heard, in response to Elfrida's prayers, was speaking, and the evil one, unwilling to lose a captive, was tightening the bonds that held a soul in thraldom. On one hand, all the power of the false religion in which he had been brought up, the lifelong habit of obedience to Leirwg, the training to subtlety and deceit, all these things seemed so many chains to hold down the soul; on the other hand, Elfrida's words, her peaceful face, and a strange, inexplicable sense that there was something higher and nobler for him than the life he was living, tugged at Osmond's heart until he felt worn and weary, and he longed for rest.

"Why should I be like this?" he asked himself. "Why cannot I be content, as in former years? My ambition has always been to please my superiors and, in time, to become a leader in religion, maybe an Arch-Druid like Leirwg. I have never thought of any other life. Why should I now begin to question and reason? But what if there is some greater God to Whom I should yield allegiance? But the thing is impossible. I can imagine the reception I should get were I to present myself to Leirwg and confess that I was no longer his humble, faithful servant, but the servant of another. It is all very well for my mother, although even for her there is a certain amount of danger, but for myself it would mean certain death. I already know too much about the practices of the priests; they would not want me to be at large with a possibility of exposure for themselves. There is no other pathway for me. I will banish these disturbing thoughts and think how best I can carry out my commission. Bernard is a disturber of the peace; it will be well that he is removed; then, the calm so rudely broken will settle down again on our souls and our lives. Alaric, Venissa, and many others will forget his words, and all will be well."

Osmond walked on as fast as the darkness and the uncertain path would permit, but it was not easy going. He had to be alert for danger: that and the thought of the work ahead of him occupied his mind for some time. After a while he found himself thinking of some words he had overheard Bernard repeat: "The way of peace have they not known." He tried to banish them from his thoughts, but it was impossible; they seemed to echo and re-echo with the sound of his footsteps.

How glad he was when the ten-mile walk, which had been set for him that night, was at an end, and he reached the home of the priest where Leirwg had given him instructions to get his first rest and to make inquiries as to whether Bernard had been seen in that neighbourhood.

Osmond could scarcely have explained why, but he felt unwilling to mention his errand to his host, and left next day without gaining any knowledge. If it had not been for the information given him so innocently by his mother, he would have been wandering aimlessly; now, depending on what she had said, he continued his journey into Gwlad-yr-hav (Somerset) and, after a few days of searching, he came upon Bernard's tracks and found that a considerable number of people had accepted his teaching. Gatherings were held every evening in various places; when the weather permitted it, the meetings were held in the open air, under the starry sky. On moonlight nights the people made their way to some secluded spot and always found Bernard ready with a message of comfort and cheer. Joy filled many hearts as they heard of the God Who loved them in spite of their sinful ways, and Who was ready to forgive sinners, and of a Saviour Who died on the Cross because of their transgressions, and Who rose again and lived for them on high.

For a while, no one seemed willing to tell Osmond the exact route to the meeting-place but, at last, professing himself to be an inquirer after the truth, Osmond persuaded a simple soul to tell him where to go. So that very evening Osmond set out on his quest. He knew he must act carefully, for Leirwg wished to capture Bernard as quietly as possible. It seemed that the wily priest realised there was a strong undercurrent of feeling against the ancient religion; many of the people were beginning to show signs of a willingness to free themselves from the old subservience to the priests, encouraged to do so by the preaching of the Gospel and by the example of the Romans who openly scorned the Druids and, more than that, had deliberately suppressed them in some places. So that from opposite motives many were showing an independent spirit annoying to the priests.

All Osmond intended doing was to gain exact details of Bernard's plans for the next few weeks, and then return to Leirwg, leaving everything in his hands. For the time being Osmond seemed to have succeeded in quieting his conflicting thoughts; he tried to persuade himself that his duty was clear, his vow of obedience still held and it was not for him to reason or question. He intended keeping out of sight, at any rate, that first evening, so he secluded himself behind a thicket and prepared to listen. He had taken longer than he had expected to do in reaching the spot and Bernard was speaking. The words that fell on Osmond's ear were those: "Come unto Me all ye that labour and are heavy laden, and I will give you rest."

Osmond heard no more. "Rest!" The word gripped him. How he longed for rest of mind. All the old conflict started again in his heart. "Rest!" He said the word to himself. Who was it that could give rest?

He crept silently away, determined that on the next day he would seek Bernard and ask of Whom he was speaking that could give rest.

Yet, when the next day came, the old teaching, the old binding ties asserted themselves once again, and Osmond hesitated. He could not act, could not determine to return to Leirwg, telling him he had found Bernard, neither did he feel he could find a trusty messenger and send tidings. He was afraid to seek Bernard, and ask for teaching; that was committing himself in a way he did not wish, but the longing for rest was such that several evenings Osmond was at the meeting place, listening eagerly to Bernard's discourses.

Meanwhile, Alaric had not forgotten the necessity of seeking Bernard and warning him of his danger. He would have started long before, but the death of Cynvelin, and Venissa's sorrow had led him to postpone his errand for a while but, at last, urged on by Venissa, he had set out to find Bernard and caution him not to return to his old haunts. Alaric had traced Bernard to Gwlad-yr-hav (Somerset) and, from various information he had gathered, felt that he was soon to find the old preacher when, walking one morning down a street in a little village, he came face to face with Osmond.

Both young men exclaimed in amazement.

"Why, Osmond, I thought you had returned to your college at Caer Isca (Exeter). Elfrida told me so," Alaric said, while Osmond remarked: "Alaric, whatever are you doing so far from home?"

Both young men hesitated. Osmond hung his head with shame at the thought of his deceit. He felt the contrast between Alaric and himself. He was struck by the manly, frank air of his friend and the charm of his peaceful countenance. Something in Osmond's manner gave Alaric a sudden idea. He spoke sternly: “Osmond, tell me truly; are you here as a spy, acting for Leirwg?”

“Alaric, oh Alaric! I don’t know what I am. I am a man torn with conflicting emotions. I have no settled foundation. The belief of my youth has left me; everything seems uncertain and I don’t know where I stand nor how to act. Let me tell you all.”

“Then, come along into the woods where we can talk in quiet,” Alaric responded, touched by Osmond’s appeal.

The two young men found a secluded spot and, seating themselves on a fallen trunk, Osmond poured forth his story. He hid nothing, and Alaric listened in grave silence as Osmond told of Leirwg’s command, and of his own unwillingness to betray Bernard, and of his longing for heart rest.

When at last he paused, Alaric said: “Osmond, no doubt God is speaking to your heart, and the devil is seeking to keep you in his service. To which will you yield? Let me beg of you to bow before God who made you, Who gave His Son to die for sinners, Who alone can forgive you your sin.”

Osmond hid his face in his hands, and groaned.

“Alaric, I have listened several evenings to Bernard’s discourses; I have heard the wonderful story of Jesus and I am convinced of the truth of all Bernard says but, alas for me! I am not a free agent, for a priest in training as I am, possessed of many of the secrets of our religion, for me it is certain death to confess Christ.”

“Do not say that, Osmond. I cannot but feel the day of the Druids’ power is almost at an end. In many places in our land the Romans have suppressed them, and it may well be that even in Devon, freedom from their pernicious rule will come before long. But if not, better to lose life itself than remain a servant of the devil, for I honestly believe that the Druids are doing the work of Satan.”

“Alaric, I am not brave like you. I am naturally timid and I know more than you do of the terrible vengeance our priests can wreak on their victims. Should I be able to stand firm? I, who am so weak?”

“God would be with you. He would uphold you, I am sure.”

The two young men sat in silence for a time, then Alaric suddenly rose from his sitting position and flung himself on his knees and prayed. He poured forth his longing for his companion's salvation; earnestly he pleaded that strength might be given to Osmond to seek Christ. When he paused and opened his eyes, Osmond was kneeling too, and with tears streaming down his face, he said: "It is settled, Alaric. I have felt the presence of God in this place. I have the conviction that He has forgiven me all the crooked, twisted ways of my past life. My hand is in His, for life or for death."

Alaric was silent from emotion. A joy too deep for words filled his heart at the thought of another soul won for the Saviour.

"Praise God," he said at last.

Together the two returned to the village and Osmond said: "Let us now find Bernard. I want to tell him of his danger and seek his counsel. I would rather throw in my lot with him."

"Do you know where to find him?" Alaric asked. "I heard from some people a few miles away from here that he was in this neighbourhood. You have guessed, I expect, that I am seeking him to warn him of the peril he is in."

"I know where he is staying, but how did you know he was threatened in any way?"

Then Alaric told Osmond of how he had chanced on the conference in the forest some weeks previously, and how he would have sought Bernard sooner had he not been delayed by Cynvelin's death.

Reaching the village, the two knocked at the door of the humble dwelling where Bernard had been staying for some weeks.

A young girl opened the door, and Alaric was struck by the look of terror in her eyes when they asked if they could have speech with Bernard.

"He has gone away," the girl answered. "He left at dawn."

"Can you tell me in which direction he went?" Alaric asked.

Without hesitation, the girl replied, "To Vindomis." (Wimborne)

"Thank you," Alaric said, and the two left, both feeling disappointed.

"It is too late to start to-day, but to-morrow we will follow him to Vindomis," both agreed.

Meanwhile, the girl watched the young men depart and then turning back into the house said to an older woman: "They were spies, I fear, seeking for Bernard, but I have put them on the wrong track. I told them he had gone to Vindomis."

"My child, how could you? You know he has returned to Devon. It was a lie you told."

The girl hung her head.

"But, grandmother, I said it to save Bernard, because I love him so."

"Bernard would rather you loved the Saviour best and sought not to grieve Him."

Poor girl, how little she knew that she had turned aside Bernard's true friends who were anxious to save him from running into the danger which lay in front of him, as he returned to Leirwg's neighbourhood.

Chapter 19.

A Narrow Escape.

"HOW did you come here?" Alaric asked, as he and Osmond turned away from the cottage. "Have you a servant with you?"

"No; I came alone and on foot. Leirwg wished me to attract no attention. I was to appear to Bernard, if I made myself known to him, as an unimportant person."

"If we are to follow Bernard to Vindomis, you will need a mount. I think the best way will be to send my attendant back; he can go on foot, and you can have his horse," Alaric replied.

"Thank you. We want to save time and reach Bernard quickly."

"But can you trust your servant? Is it wise to let him know I am with you?" Osmond inquired, ever timid and cautious.

"Yes; indeed, I can. He is one of us. I can explain the position to him. He will be as silent as the grave."

"That is well. We must start at dawn, so now to rest," Osmond answered.

The two young men grew very friendly, as they journeyed together. Alaric, somewhat to his own surprise, found himself telling Osmond of his love for Venissa.

Osmond warmly approved of Alaric's intentions, and was surprised when Alaric said, "I doubt if Venissa returns my love."

"Nonsense, my lad. That is just humility on your part. Why! have you not been the greatest of friends from childhood? Venissa never seems happier than when she is with you."

"I know that, but she looks on me as a brother."

"Well, it will be for you to teach her to look on you as a lover. I am sure you can win her. I doubt if she has thought of love in the sense of which we are speaking, her pleasure in your society gives you a good start. I could not help noticing the other day when I saw you going off to the woods together, how bright Venissa looked. It seemed as if for the time being she had forgotten her sorrow and I rejoiced, for I am very fond of my cousin, and I have felt pained at her grief at the loss of her father."

"Oh, did you see us? We were going up to old Griselda's hut. Venissa has a fancy for keeping it in order. We light a fire there occasionally and keep it dry. It is quite habitable. Venissa seems to feel that some one will need it some day."

Most of the conversation, however, was on the matter of Osmond's return and of the confession he would have to make to Leirwg. Alaric made a suggestion that perhaps Osmond would like to remain with Bernard when they found him, but Osmond said: "Think of the joy it will be to my mother when she knows that her prayers are answered and the Saviour has found me."

"But you will have a wily, dangerous foe to face. Remember Cynvelin."

"I do, and at times I am full of fear, but I must witness to my faith in Christ and trust Him to protect me. He is able, and if I am called to suffer I believe He will not fail to give me strength."

Alaric was struck with the change in Osmond; already he was growing strong in faith, and Alaric rejoiced at what grace could do in a heart yielded to Christ.

For some days the two travelled, sometimes missing their way, for roads, save for the great Roman roads, were non-existent, and most of the land was thickly wooded. They meant to make straight for Vindomis, (Wimborne) but found themselves further south, nearer Caer Wyn (Winchester), where the Romans had a camp. They were in the neighbourhood one morning, and drew rein on a hill overlooking a steep descent.

"Rather a sudden dip," Alaric remarked. "Keep your horse well under control. I should not like to let my steed rush headlong down. Why, look—"

He broke off his speech, pointing to a figure coming towards them. A rider was dashing along at a tremendous rate, and making straight for the precipice.

"The horse has run away," Osmond said.

"Here, take my reins." Alaric flung himself off and prepared, as the horse came near, to spring at the bridle and check its mad career.

Osmond held his breath, for it was a risky thing to do. The thundering hoofs pounding on the hard soil sounded like a death knell. There was just time to note that the rider was a young Roman soldier, the horse a black, handsome steed with eyes that showed the whites, and with ears turned back. Alaric sprang, held on for dear life, was dragged a few yards, then the steady pressure told; the animal slowed up and, just before the precipice was reached, stood still trembling in every limb.

The rider flung himself off with an exclamation of horror, as he saw how near the brink they were. Alaric was very white, but otherwise gave no sign of exhaustion. In his young, strong manhood, every muscle firm, sound in brain and brawn, he was well fitted to stand strain and stress.

"How can I thank you for your timely aid?" the newcomer said, speaking the British language with a foreign accent, and then to the joy and amazement of both Alaric and Osmond, he continued:
"I thank my Heavenly Father that He sent you in the nick of time for my preservation."

"Then, you are one of us," Alaric exclaimed.

"Does that mean you have learnt to know the one true God and worship Him?" the young Roman soldier asked.

"Yes, indeed," both Alaric and Osmond answered, Osmond adding: "It was only two weeks ago that I found the Lord, and you?" he asked.

"I have known the Saviour for some few years; partly through my father, Felicius, and partly through my mother's slave, Sigma. You are travellers, I see. Can I offer you hospitality? We are only about five miles from my home. My father is in charge of a Roman cavalry unit, and we are stationed at Caer Wyn. We arrived here from Rome only about ten days ago, but we spent some years in this land in my boyhood. We were living then at Aqua Solis, so you see I feel quite at home in Britain."

"Thank you, we shall be glad to accept your kind offer. We are making for Vindomis, but have, we fear, struck too southerly a track. Perhaps you can give us directions."

"I fear not, as I have not had time to explore the neighbourhood yet, but as you are returning with me we can make inquiries, and if you will spend the night at our villa, you can start fresh at dawn."

So the three rode on together until they reached Marcus's home.

When Felicius and Placidia heard of the deliverance from danger of their son, they welcomed the young men warmly, Felicius especially so when he found that they served the same Master as himself.

The four men sat talking until late that night, seeking to encourage one another in the faith. Alaric and Osmond told of their quest for Bernard, and Felicius and Marcus assured them that if Bernard came to Caer Wyn, they would afford him protection and give him their aid in his work of spreading the Gospel. Before Alaric and Osmond left, they gave Marcus a hearty invitation to visit them in Devon, and Marcus replied: "I have always wanted to visit that part of the land. Its very name draws me, -'The land of the deep dales.' I shall come along some day, without doubt."

"And you will find us ready to receive you," both young men assured him.

After a few days spent in Vindomis and the neighbourhood, Alaric and Osmond began to despair of finding Bernard; no one had seen any one at all answering to the description they gave. They decided they must return home, although extremely disappointed at the failure of their mission.

They went out of their way to call at Caer Wyn and let Felicius and Marcus know that they had not succeeded in their search, so had been unable to give Bernard Felicius' kind invitation to settle at Caer Wyn. Both Felicius and Marcus promised to keep a look out for the old preacher and would also instruct their soldiers to do the same.

"If he is anywhere within a radius of twenty miles, we shall find him," Marcus assured his friends.

So Alaric and Osmond turned their faces homeward, both feeling grave as they knew Osmond must be prepared for persecution and ignominy.

Alaric tried to keep Osmond from dwelling unduly on what awaited him. He felt that for Osmond, with his naturally timid disposition, the anticipation of a trial was often the hardest part to bear, so he discussed their new friends at length. They were favourably impressed by the Roman family. Felicius, with his courtesy; Marcus' frank manly bearing; Placidia too had been all smiles and graciousness, and as for Canace, Osmond said: "What a charming girl she is, so gentle and sweet. I think she will make a beautiful woman, don't you think so, Alaric?"

Alaric agreed somewhat absentmindedly; for at the moment he was thinking of Venissa.

Chapter 20.

A Brave Deed

THE days were long and sad to Venissa in her shadowed home. Her father had always been so much to her; it was he who, from her earliest days, had been her hero, her ideal of all that was noble and good. Now that he was gone, Venissa was constantly thinking over the scenes of her childhood, recalling her father's wise counsel and sometimes loving reproof, and the real friendship which had existed between father and daughter in later years.

At times the faith so recently planted in her heart triumphed, and she realised that her father was safe in the keeping of the Saviour she had learnt to love. She was very ignorant, knowing so little of spiritual matters, and she longed for the presence of Bernard that she might hear from him comforting words, but felt that desire would not be gratified, for had not Alaric gone to warn him not to return to Devon.

Little Julia was a constant solace to her, for the child talked so simply of Jesus the Good Shepherd, saying: "The Good Shepherd will take care of us, Venissa, won't He?" She spoke of Cynvelin as being with Jesus. "He is so happy there," she often said. Little Julia had no doubts and her simplicity and love brought comfort to Venissa's sorrowing heart.

It was not only the loss of her father that caused Venissa grief, but also that Hulda's condition was a source of anxiety. She seemed so changed, her face was growing lined and her eyes wild. She would sit brooding for hours at a stretch, only rousing herself when Leirwg visited her, which he did frequently. Venissa saw with dismay that Hulda was completely under the priest's sway; what he ordered, she did. Venissa's advice or suggestions were ignored. She felt she must try to help her mother to shake off this bondage, and one day spoke seriously to her on the matter. She suggested that surely it was not necessary to ask his advice on every subject, even to the management of the household slaves. A look of terror came into the older woman's eyes, as she answered: "I must, I must obey him. It is only he who stands between us and the wrath of the gods. Remember what happened to your poor father, because in his madness he turned away from the old worship."

"Mother, dearest, don't let Leirwg completely control you. You always were able to act for yourself. Why, who knows what he may ask you to do next? He may even command you to give me in sacrifice."

Hulda gave a shriek of anguish, and fell in a faint on the floor. Poor Venissa was distressed, indeed, and she took care never to mention again the horrible thought that was so often in her own mind. Now that Bernard, Alaric and Osmond were all at a distance, she felt her loneliness and unprotected condition sorely.

One day about noon Venissa was returning from a visit to Elfrida, whose faith and joy in the Lord had helped to cheer and encourage the poor girl. She was walking along a woodland track when she espied someone seated on a mossy bank. Even at a distance she realised the attitude of weariness that characterised the traveller.

"Who is it, I wonder?" she thought, for the face was turned away, and yet she felt there was something familiar about the figure. Then, as she drew nearer, she exclaimed with a throb of joy, "It's Bernard!"

Her next thought was one of dismay. Bernard back again, where Leirwg held sway and where Bernard's life was not worth the smallest bronze coin. She hastened forward, and Bernard's face lit with pleasure as he saw who was coming.

"Oh, Bernard, why are you here? Alaric went to warn you to keep away from this neighbourhood," Venissa said, alarm in her voice.

"I have not seen him, my child. Come and sit beside me, and tell me all the news."

So Venissa told him of her father's death, and her suspicion which Alaric shared. Bernard's dark eyes flashed for a moment with indignation, then he said softly: "Venissa, your father has won a martyr's crown; he died for his faith."

"That is what Alaric said, but, oh, Bernard, how I miss him!"

It was with a struggle that Venissa restrained her tears.

"Fret not, my child. We shall go to him, and remember, God is the Father of the fatherless. Tell me about your mother. Has she received Christ? Is she one of us? I hoped at one time she was interested in the good news and inclined to give up false gods and surrender to the one true God."

"Alas, Bernard! She is more zealous than ever in the old religion. She is guided by Leirwg entirely. I feel whatever he commands, she will do."

"Ah, that is sad! The good seed has been snatched away by the evil one, or choked by the cares of life."

"But, Bernard, what I am concerned about now is your safety. How can I help you? How can I hide you from Leirwg until Alaric returns? You see, it is like this. Alaric found out that Leirwg has determined to put you to death; he is so angry because so many have turned from idols and false gods; he says it is through your teaching, which we know is true. That is why Alaric went to try and find you to give you warning not to return. When he comes back he will know what is best to do, but meanwhile, I must do something to shield you."

"Do not fear for me, my child. I am in my Father's hands. I came back because I longed to know how the young in the faith were getting on. I realise the need of giving nourishment and teaching to those who have come to know Christ as their Saviour."

Venissa was thoughtful, then she exclaimed: "I know what I can do. I must take you to old Griselda's hut. You will be safe there. Everyone is terrified of going near that spot, thinking it is haunted by evil spirits. I must return home now, or my mother will be sending to look for me; she is so nervous lately that if I am delayed she thinks something terrible has happened to me. I think she fears Leirwg will capture and hide me. Can you shelter in that thicket and keep hidden? I will come again as soon as I can and lead you to the hut. Alaric and I were there only a short time ago; we lit a fire and dried the rugs. I will bring food with me, and there is a spring of water near and all that you will need for a time."

"My child, it is indeed good of you to think out a plan for me like this, but I must not turn my back on danger thus."

"Oh, please, please do as I say, at any rate until Alaric comes home."

Bernard hesitated. It was doubtful if he would have yielded to Venissa's pleading, but he was feeling utterly spent; besides which he saw it would distress Venissa if he lingered where Leirwg could get hold of him. Venissa continued her arguments.

"Bernard, I can let those who love you know, and we can come and visit you for teaching. Those of us who love the Saviour will not be afraid to come; we know God is our Guard from all evil."

So Bernard consented. Then, Venissa asked when he had last had food, and exclaimed joyfully: "Why, I am forgetting. I have some oatcakes here. My Aunt Elfrida gave them to me for Julia; she is very fond of the kind which aunt makes. Julia would give them to you willingly, if she were asked."

"Thank you. I would not take them, but I am in sore need of refreshment. I have not broken my fast today. Tell me, how is the child?"

"Not very well. She has had a touch of fever. I tried to hide it from my mother, and truly mother scarcely notices the little one nowadays, she is so changed in every way, but I was afraid if mother knew Julia was not well she would ask Leirwg for medicine, and I am frightened of anything he might give."

"I am glad you have told me, my child. I will pray for the child and, doubtless, you know remedies that are suitable."

"Yes, I have given her herbs, and our woman, Amelia, is very clever; she understands how to treat a child. Julia is better today. Now, I must go. Do keep out of sight until I return."

Venissa was not able to get back to Bernard as soon as she had hoped. Leirwg was with her mother and, until he left the house, she felt unable to set forth. He might quite easily suspect her movements, if he saw her go out with a basket on her arm, although he probably knew she frequented the dwellings of the poor and gave assistance. Since the love of Christ had come into her heart she lost no opportunity of doing good and, at the same time, telling the story of the good news of the Saviour and His sacrifice for needy, sinful souls. So, though it was possible Leirwg would only think she was going on some ordinary errand of mercy, Venissa was nervous lest Leirwg should, with his remarkable powers of penetration, guess her intentions. Several times she and Alaric had remarked how Leirwg seemed to know, without being told, what they were about to do. It puzzled them; Alaric wondered whether the devil, whom Leirwg served, sometimes gave the man a horrible discernment, while Venissa thought it possible that he possessed mental ability and shrewdness beyond the majority of mankind. Whichever was right, it made both of them afraid of Leirwg and cautious in his presence.

It was late in the afternoon before Leirwg left, and Venissa hastily filled a wicker basket with food and a bronze tankard with nourishing broth, and slipped away to their meeting-place.

She found Bernard feeling very faint, and at first she wondered whether he could manage the long, rough walk. How glad she was she had brought the broth; it was still hot, and she poured some into a little wooden bowl, beautifully fashioned and decorated with carving, which she had brought with her.

Bernard drank gratefully, and the nourishment revived him, so together they started on their journey. Bernard offered to carry the basket, but Venissa would not allow him to do so. She laughed and told him that truly she was well able to bear a burden. Every British girl, of whatever station in life, was used to work which developed the muscles, and Venissa was no shirker.

Bernard asked, as they walked along: "Was it easy for you to get away, my child? I began to think something had delayed you."

"Yes, that was so. Leirwg was in our house, so I waited until he had left. My mother has retired to her room with a headache. She told me she was not to be disturbed by anyone today so, fortunately, she will not miss me."

It took a long time to reach the hiding place, for Bernard had to pause for breath after every steep climb, but at last they were at their destination. Bernard suggested that Venissa should at once start for home, but she insisted on lighting the fire before she left; it was a good thing that Alaric had provided the hut with twigs on his last visit, also branches of trees, so there was kindling matter to hand as well as a flint-striker and a lump of iron pyrites.[10] As soon as Venissa had a cheery fire going, she unpacked the basket, arranged the low couch with rugs, and prepared to leave. Before she took her departure, Bernard knelt in prayer, thanking God for sending Venissa to his aid and commending her to God's care for the homeward journey.

"If I cannot come again soon, there are others who will," Venissa said. "There are so many who love you, and, loving the Saviour, they will have no fear of this spot; while those who still serve false gods and live in terror of evil spirits will keep away."

---

[10] The forerunner of flint and steel

"Thank you, my child, for all you have done for me. I do feel the need of a rest and am grateful for this peaceful place. Send those who have received the message along, that I may know how they prosper in the faith. Tell me, how is that young slave of yours doing? Hubert, I believe, is his name."

"Splendidly. He has received Christ as his Saviour, and is a real comfort to me. I should have brought him with me today, but my mother had appointed him a task which would take him all day to finish, and it would have aroused suspicion had I asked that he might be excused."

"I do not like you going back alone, my child, but I must trust you to our Heavenly Father's care. Good-bye. God bless you."

So Venissa turned her footsteps homeward. It was dark now and she shivered at the thought of the perils in her path. She whispered a prayer for help and protection as she hurried along. It was not possible to run, for the track was rough, and roots of trees, brambles, and thick undergrowth impeded her steps, but she pressed on, starting occasionally as sounds of night animals began to increase. So long as it was only a fox, a hare or some other harmless creature crossing her path or rustling away at the noise of her approach, she did not mind, but all her senses were alert for the dreaded howl of the wolf or the stealthy drawing near of the wild cat, from either of which there was real danger.

She was about half-way home when the horrible drawn-out howl she had feared was heard, and Venissa knew the wolves were out. Her heart thumped, but in spite of natural fear, she looked up to her Father in Heaven for protection, and was comforted.

Presently, she saw the gleam of eyes in her pathway; she could not turn aside, the bushes being too thick to admit of that. She stood still, and those awful eyes seemed fixed on her. All the stories she had heard from childhood of the werewolf flashed into her mind. Suppose it was not a real wolf! Suppose Leirwg had the power to change himself into a wolf, as her old nurse and others had always told her certain people had the power to do. For a moment she was paralysed with fright. Then, suddenly the story which Bernard had told her of how God had protected Daniel from the lions came into her mind. And was not God just the same today? Fear fled, and she lifted up her voice in song.

"Christ is my Refuge in times of distress,
Christ is my Saviour when enemies press.
Fearless I trust Him to still my alarm;
Safely He keeps with His sheltering arm."

The wolf turned and trotted silently away. Venissa went on and, although she heard the distant howls of the fierce animals, not one came near her again, and before the household had retired to rest, before the stockade was secured against night visitors, Venissa was safely at home. Hulda was still in her room so wrapped in her own sorrows and fears that she had not thought of Venissa; at any rate, no one had seen anything of the mistress, and the servants, being accustomed to Venissa's absence at times, made no comment.

Little Julia was fast asleep. Venissa stooped over the child, and kissed her before she sought her own bed.

Chapter 21

Osmond's Confession

ALARIC and Osmond were inclined to linger on their homeward journey. For one reason, they still sought for Bernard, thinking probably he had stopped in some village to preach the Gospel on his way to Vindomis (Wimborne). They both longed for an interview with him, for their own benefit as well as his, for spiritual conversation and also to give Bernard the warning. Then, too, Osmond feared Leirwg's wrath; it was not easy to go forward to what seemed likely to be fierce persecution; although still steadfast in his purpose to return and witness a good confession, yet there was the shrinking of the flesh from suffering and reproach which was almost certain to be meted out to him.

But at last they gave up the quest and made their way home. While Osmond went to his mother, Alaric sought Venissa. He found her among the maidens superintending the dyeing of goats' hair and sheep's wool. Alaric paused a moment, as he stood at a little distance thinking he had never seen Venissa looking more attractive. Her face had lost its childish contour, and her eyes were more thoughtful than formerly, for the trial she had passed through and the responsibility which was now hers had made a difference both to her countenance and her character, but the sweet seriousness of her manner was very engaging, at any rate in Alaric's eyes.

Presently, Venissa turned her eyes in his direction. "Oh, Alaric, you have returned!" she said. An ordinary remark, but there was no mistaking the real pleasure in her tone. It brought a thrill of joy to Alaric's heart. Giving directions to the maidens to continue their work, Venissa led Alaric to a quiet room where they could converse without being overheard. Julia came running to meet them, exclaiming: "Venissa, may I dye my baby's gown, it is so shabby?"

Venissa smiled, as Julia held up her wooden doll for inspection.

"Of course, you may, darling. Take it to Amelia and ask her to help you. But are you not going to greet Alaric first?" Julia held up her face for a kiss, saying, "I'm glad you've come," but her thoughts were on the matter of dyeing and she asked: "Which colour shall I choose?" "You will find a lovely shade of blue from the woad," Venissa answered. "Oh, Venissa! Blue is only for the slaves." "But it is a pretty colour. I think it is a pity we may not wear it, but there is purple from the whortle-berries, will that do?" "Yes, that is royal, and my baby is a real princess." Alaric and Venissa both laughed, for the battered shabby, wooden doll looked anything but aristocratic. "A princess in disguise perhaps," Alaric said, as Julia ran off to the dyeing ground.

As soon as the two were seated, Alaric said: "Venissa, I have failed to find Bernard. I am distressed for fear some evil has befallen him."

"He is here, Alaric."

"Here! In this house!"

"Oh, no! I have taken him to Griselda's hut. Only those who love him and have received the Gospel know that he is in the neighbourhood. We take him food and one by one hear words of help and comfort from his lips. It is quite easy for us to visit him frequently without suspicion, for at this time of the year we are gathering the lichens for dyeing and the elderberries and sloes for making our winter drinks. We take our baskets with food for him and return laden with our spoils. But, Alaric, he is very frail. His journeyings have wearied him, and he is glad to rest; perhaps, that is a good thing, for otherwise he would not be content to stay there; he is so keen on spreading the Gospel where it is not already known."

"I am indeed relieved to hear he is safe. If we can persuade him to remain there, he will get the rest he needs, but one never knows whether he will not think it is his duty to be off with the good news, as you say. Truly, he does not consider himself, if only he can tell of Christ. Venissa, who do you think joined me in the search for Bernard?"

"I cannot tell," Venissa answered with a little puzzled frown on her forehead.

"Osmond."

"Osmond! Oh, Alaric! But he was trying to betray him to Leirwg; at least, that was what I feared."

"He was sent forth with that purpose, but when he had found Bernard, he spent several evenings in listening to the message, keeping himself hidden among those who crowded round to hear, and the result is that Osmond is now a believer."

"How glad Aunt Elfrida will be! She is praying for Osmond's conversion."

After a moment's reflection, Venissa added with dismay in her tone: "But, Alaric, Leirwg will excommunicate him."

"I fear he will," Alaric answered gravely. To himself he thought: "I hope Leirwg will not do worse than that."

"Osmond is so happy," he continued. "He finds the terrible unrest and fear he experienced have gone. He is at peace and is praying for grace to suffer for Christ's sake. And you, Venissa, how have you been getting on and how is your mother?"

Venissa answered the latter part of the question.

"Mother is so changed. She seems like a woman haunted. Sometimes I fear for her reason; her bondage to Leirwg is shocking; she refuses to decide anything without asking his opinion. He practically rules in our house and among our servants; and yet, in spite of him, several of our slaves have received the good news. I dare not let mother know this, but the Gospel spreads and it has brought peace to many a burdened heart."

"How splendid! And is Leirwg taking no steps to enforce the practices of the old religion?"

"No. I cannot understand his apparent indifference. Of course, we were always allowed to be a bit slack between the great festivals; the testing time will come when the sacred days come again. I am so glad you are at home, Alaric. I feel so much safer when you are near."

Alaric's heart bounded with pleasure and his eyes shone.

"Dear heart, it is good to have your welcome."

He paused, and wondered whether the time had come to ask Venissa to be his but, at that moment, Hulda came into the room. Her greeting was cool; it was evident she did not desire Alaric's presence; so with a sigh of regret he left the house. In spite of a frown on her mother's face, Venissa accompanied her friend to the outer gate, for she wanted to know how soon Alaric would be able to visit Bernard and to make sure that he would take a supply of food to the old preacher. Being assured on that point, Venissa returned to her mother, who began at once to remonstrate with her daughter.

"Venissa, you must not encourage Alaric to come here. Leirwg does not approve of your friendship."

"Mother, are we to be controlled entirely by what Leirwg wishes? Dear father loved Alaric, and wished me to be guided by him."

"Peace, child; you do not seem to understand. Leirwg tells me of the awful wrath of the gods which will fall upon you as it did on your poor father if you do not obey him. It is for your safety and welfare that Leirwg is working. Alaric is setting the religion of his forefathers at nought; no good can come from such misguided behaviour."

Venissa sighed. It was useless discussing the state of affairs with her mother, so she introduced another topic.

"Mother, I hear Osmond is at home again."

"So soon! Well, it will give Elfrida pleasure. I suppose it is only a brief visit?"

"Mother, you will have to know, so I may as well tell you. Osmond has learnt to love the Saviour."

Hulda turned puzzled eyes on her daughter.

"What do you mean, child?"

"You know, the One of Whom Bernard has taught us, the Saviour in Whom father trusted before he died"

Hulda broke into a wail of anguish.

"Venissa, Venissa, who has bewitched you all? Judgement will fall upon us if so many around persist in this folly. Alas, alas! My husband, my child, my sister, and, now, my nephew ! For him it is the greatest tragedy of all, for was he not a priest of the old religion? There is nothing but disaster ahead. Alas, alas!"

"Mother, darling, do not fear. Do not bewail us thus. God Whom we worship and seek to serve is the one true God to Whom all power belongs. He is able to keep us from harm."

"But, Venissa, have not some who have embraced this religion been put to death because of it? Leirwg tells me so, and I think I have heard Bernard say so also."

"Yes, mother, that is so; but those who have suffered thus have rejoiced that they were counted worthy to suffer for His Name and grace was given to them to endure."

"You don't know what you are talking about, you foolish child. How I wish that man Bernard had never come to this neighbourhood! One thing I am glad of, that he has disappeared and no one seems to know where he has gone."

Venissa was silent, glad to feel that her mother was in ignorance of Bernard's presence in the hut on the hills.

At the same time Alaric was talking with Venissa, Osmond was with his mother who could not express her joy at what he told her.

"Mother, your prayers are answered! I have learnt to love the Saviour," he said, after she had exclaimed in surprise at his appearance, thinking that he had returned to his college at Caer Isca (Exeter)and was not likely to come home for some months.

"My boy, my boy! What can I say? God has done more for me than I dared to hope. I was thinking that at some distant day, perhaps, when I was gone and you an old man, you would learn how futile, how deceptive the worship of false gods is, and turn to the Saviour. But now, while you are young and strong, you are His. Praise, praise be to His Name! Tell me all about it, and how it came to pass."

Then Osmond told her how he had been sent to track Bernard; to let Leirwg know of the old man's whereabouts, and how Leirwg had evil designs against him.

At the mention of Leirwg's name, Elfrida shivered. She realised what it might mean when her son made his confession to the Arch-Druid, but she lifted her heart to God with a voiceless cry for strength and grace for herself and her son, while Osmond continued:

"My heart was sad, mother, as I went forth; I had for months been feeling the falsity of our old religion. Then, when I had found Bernard, I managed to be an unseen listener several evenings at his meetings, and the words he spoke took hold of me, especially when he repeated the words that the Lord Jesus Himself spoke: 'Come unto Me all ye that labour and are heavy laden, and I will give you rest!' Mother, there is no rest for us, apart from the Saviour. There is no cleansing apart from the Blood which He shed for us. There is no forgiveness save through Him."

"My boy, those are the same words that attracted me, the first evening that Bernard told us of the love of God and the rest that He alone could give. I now rejoice in that rest, that forgiveness; we can praise God together."

Osmond rose from his stool and said: "Mother, I must go to Leirwg and report myself; the sooner I get the interview over the better. I now hope to break off the shackles of Druidism and be free to come and live with you, and relieve you of the responsibilities that press upon you. Pray for me that I may have strength to witness to Leirwg, and to brave his scorn and anger."

"I will, my boy. I shall continue in prayer until you return. God protect you. I fear that man greatly."

Osmond had to wait some time before he gained admittance to Leirwg's presence. When at last he was ushered into the great man's room, he was conscious that he was received with cold disapproval.

"So you have returned! Did you not understand my instructions, that you were to find Bernard and not lose sight of him but send me a message? Am I to gather that you have failed to find him or that, finding him, you have foolishly left him and returned here?"

"Sir, I found him and, finding him, I listened to his message. It fell upon my troubled spirit, and brought me rest. I no longer believe in the false gods I had been taught to worship. I no longer fear them nor evil spirits. I have learnt to know the one true God and His Son, Jesus Christ, Who died for me and in my stead."

Osmond paused; he was trembling in every limb, for the confession was not made without cost. There was dead silence; then, Osmond spoke again; he realised that he had something more to say.

"In consequence of my changed views, I wish to be released from the remaining time of my training. I cannot return to college."

Again Osmond waited. Would Leirwg strike him to the ground? Would he curse him? What would he do? Osmond had been standing with bowed head; now he ventured to look at the priest. Leirwg's face was inscrutable; it was impossible to tell what his thoughts were.

Quietly he spoke at last. "I am bitterly disappointed, Osmond. You were a promising pupil. Go and do not let me see your face again. You are a fool, ensnared by a few fair words from that worthless old man. Go; give up all your prospect of being a great man among your people. Go to your mother, sink into a mere country man of the soil. I wash my hands of you. Go!"

Leirwg thundered out the last word, and turned his back on Osmond, who quickly retired wondering greatly at being let off so easily.

Left alone, Leirwg's face became distorted with an evil passion. He shook his fist at the retreating figure and muttered: "Wait a bit, my lad. My plans are not matured yet. I'll deal with you later, and bitterly you shall rue the day you rejected the old religion; you, and some others. Ah, I haven't done with you yet. I can afford to wait."

Osmond was not the only one puzzled, as the days passed and Leirwg seemed to accept Osmond's desertion so calmly. Elfrida, Alaric and Venissa, and others wondered at it, and some of them decided that the old man was growing more tolerant with advancing years.

Meanwhile, the Gospel spread; hymns were sung openly, and apparently Leirwg was indifferent. It was a time of peace and rest, and only a few feared it might be a lull before a storm.

Chapter 22.

The Visit Of Marcus.

"MARCUS, my son, I want to send you into the western lands on an expedition. I have orders from Rome to make a survey of that part of the country. You know that copper and tin ore are to be found there and many metal-smelting communities are established in the west. The tin, after it is purified, is carried to the island of Ictis (St. Michael's Mount) which is only accessible at low tide, and from thence it is shipped to Gaul and carried overland on pack-horses. It seems that the trade could be developed profitably and, as I am needed in this district, I am entrusting this commission to you."

"I will do my best to gain all the information possible" replied Marcus. In order to reach Dumnonii (Cornwall) I must travel through

Devon. With your permission I will use the opportunity to visit the young man, Alaric, whom you remember we entertained some weeks ago, and who kindly invited me to come to his home at any time."

"Certainly, my boy. You can put in a few days with him, either on your outward journey or when returning home, whichever seems most convenient. Now which of the men will you take with you? I should suggest at least six. Travel is not without its peril these days, and I should like to feel you were well equipped for emergencies. You must take tents and all that you will need for some weeks of absence. Food, doubtless, you can obtain as you go."

Felicius proceeded to name the men he thought most reliable for the expedition, and only a few days passed before Marcus said farewell to his father, Placidia, his mother, and his sisters, Canace and Flora.

"What shall I bring you?" Marcus asked his sisters.

"A necklace of British beads, please," Canace said without hesitation.

Marcus smiled. "I shall be able to get them at Caer Isca, I expect. Do you want them of glass, amber, or bronze, or perhaps jet?"

"Glass, please. Mother has some and they are so pretty, but I have none of my own."

"And you, Flora; what will you have?"

"A little British slave girl."

Canace spoke quickly. "Oh, Flora, have you forgotten what Sigma told us: that those who love Jesus and want to please Him, do not have slaves?"

Flora pouted.

"Well, mother has them."

This was an unanswerable argument, and Canace was silent while Marcus said: "I'll bring you an enamel brooch; you will like that."

Flora was easily pleased. She clapped her hands, saying happily, "That will be lovely."

When Marcus was gone, Flora reverted to her request.

"Canace, I do want a little girl to play with; you are so big!"

Canace laughed: "I can't help that. I wish we had never lost our little Julia," she added in a wistful tone. "You would have had her to play with. Do you remember her, Flora?"

"I think I do. She used to call me 'Ora', didn't she?"

"She was such a darling baby but, hush, don't talk about her to mother; she is coming, and it makes her sad to think about Julia."

Marcus enjoyed every mile of his journey. The crisp, autumnal air was pleasant to him; the tint of the leaves on the trees, in all their varying shades from gold to bronze, delighted his eye, and all went well on the journey. After a few days had passed, he arrived in the neighbourhood of Alaric's home, and soon found his way there.

He was welcomed by Alaric and his old father, and urged to stay several days. There was ample room for his six attendants, and his horses. So Marcus willingly accepted the invitation. He and Alaric had much in common. Both loved the Saviour and so were able to help one another. Alaric knew more of the teaching of the Bible, for he had had the advantage of some months of instruction from Bernard, while Marcus had had only occasional opportunities of hearing God's Word at a gathering in the Catacombs.

Marcus had not long been with Alaric before he remarked: "I have kept a look out for the old teacher, as you asked me to do, but I have neither seen nor heard anything of him."

"No, because I was misled in seeking him at Vindomis. He had returned here."

"Indeed, and has he been kept in safety? You feared persecution for him, did you not?"

"We did. But we have found a safe hiding place for him. There is an old hut hidden in the woods about three miles from here; it is a safe refuge because it has an evil reputation. Most people think it is a haunted spot; in fact, we all thought so until the Gospel reached us; now, those of us who know and love Christ no longer have foolish fears, so we go to Bernard and listen to his helpful words. Would you like to visit him?"

"Indeed, I would", Marcus answered.

So next day, taking with them fishing tackle, so that no unfriendly person might suspect them of any other motive than a day of sport, they made their way there. They went by rather a devious path, as Alaric wanted to show Marcus some of the beauty spots of the neighbourhood. Marcus was entranced with the wide stretches of moorland, the rugged tors, the deep dales and winding streams. They walked a good many miles, and it was noon before they reached the hut. They heard the sound of voices as they drew near and, as they emerged from the thick woodland into the little clearing, they stood still watching for a few moments the scene before them, pausing awhile, unwilling to make themselves visible to the two figures seated outside the hut.

Marcus thought he had seldom seen a more charming sight, and Alaric, although both were so well known to him, would certainly have expressed a similar thought if he had spoken.

The old preacher was seated on a bench. His long white beard, snowy hair, and deep, dark eyes made him a striking sight; while on the ground, at his feet, sat Venissa, dressed in a long white tunic, over which was thrown a soft leather cape of well-dressed deer skin, fastened on the shoulder with two bronze buttons; her long plaits of hair, now a little darker than formerly, were hanging down her back, and her sweet face was upturned to the old preacher as she listened to what he was saying. At a little distance could be seen Venissa's young servant, Hubert, who was collecting firewood for the replenishing of Bernard's store.

Suddenly, Bernard looked in the direction where Alaric and Marcus stood, and said: "Who have we here?"

Before Venissa could reply, he continued: "It is our good friend, Alaric, so doubtless the one with him is also a friend."

Alaric at once introduced Marcus and they all sat together round their old teacher.

"Will you tell Alaric and Marcus what you were telling me?" Venissa said.

"Certainly, my child, if our friends wish it."

"Please do," Marcus said eagerly. "Alaric has been telling me of the helpful teaching you have given him. I have had little opportunity of hearing of God. I shall be glad to be taught more."

"I was telling Venissa of an instance in the days when the world was young. I was reading it only recently in the Holy Scriptures."

"Oh, can you read?" Marcus asked.

"Yes, I can read Greek. I lived in Athens some years ago when I was a young man, and I studied a great deal, especially the different religions. I was never attracted by the Epicureans, but I was inclined to become a disciple of those who followed the philosopher Zeno in his teaching. Then, at one time, I was a Stoic; finally, I came in contact with a follower of Jesus Christ, and I learnt to know Him Who died to make an atonement for sinners, and ever since He revealed His love to me, I have had one burning desire, to point others to Him that they, too, might be saved."

"As I was saying just now, I was telling Venissa of a happening in the life of Abram; he was a man whom God called out from the heathen to become the father of the nation chosen by God as His own special people. One day it happened that Abram had been engaged in a great battle against five kings in order to rescue his nephew, Lot. Abram was victorious, but such conquests are not won save at the cost of strength of nerve and brawn. Returning, doubtless, weary, the priest of God met him with bread and wine and blessing. This is the first mention of a priest in the Holy Scriptures, and it is significant that he is presented as one succouring and blessing a servant of God, bread to strengthen, wine to cheer, and the blessing of God resting on Abram. I would direct your thoughts to the Great High Priest of Whom this ancient priest Melchisedec was a type. Our High Priest lives to care for and to bless us today. He, too, knows the feebleness of our frames and the battle of life; He often comes to meet us in spirit with the Bread of Life."

Bernard paused, and Marcus said thoughtfully: "I do not quite understand. Are you speaking of the Lord Jesus? I have heard of Him as Saviour and Lord. I believe He is my Saviour and I worship Him as my Lord, but I have never heard of Him as High Priest."

"Yes, my young friend," Bernard said. "Let me read to you what the Scriptures say about Christ as High Priest."

Bringing from the hut his treasured parchments, Bernard read to his listeners, and then explained the texts. Four of them were thoughtfully heeding the words now, for the young slave Hubert had drawn near and, at a gesture from Venissa, had seated himself just behind his mistress and was listening attentively.

Reluctantly, at last, Venissa said she must be going home. Marcus accompanied Bernard into the hut, carrying the parchment rolls which fascinated the young Roman; he lingered a few moments examining them, and Alaric and Venissa stood talking together.

Alaric asked: "Shall I bring Marcus to see your mother, Venissa?"

To his surprise, Venissa replied: "I would rather not. I hate to be inhospitable, but mother is so, so—well not herself nowadays. I never know what is going to upset her, and she is so opposed to any one who is a Christian. She would be sure to ask this about your friend, and at once become antagonistic to him. Oh, Alaric, life is so full of burdens; it seems years ago that I was happy and carefree in dear father's days but, there, I ought not to talk like that; it is faithless. I have a deep peace to which I was a stranger then, and I know I am under my loving Heavenly Father's care."

"Yes, indeed, dear. I wish I could share your burdens. Can you not —?"

Whatever Alaric was about to say was interrupted, for Marcus joined them and they all went off together. Venissa was surprised to find how easy it was to talk to Marcus. She could scarcely believe they had only met for the first time that day. She saw him once again before he went on his expedition to Dumnonii (Cornwall), promising to pay another visit on his return journey. Alaric said he must make a longer stay then but when, after a few weeks, Marcus did come back to that neighbourhood, he felt he must not linger except for one night, as he thought he had been away longer than his father had anticipated and he would be expecting his son back. On that visit Venissa did not see him.

When he reached home, Marcus was able to give a satisfactory report of his investigation. His father was pleased with his straightforward account of the business he had undertaken. Canace and Flora were delighted with their presents, but Placidia studied her son and felt that he was somewhat absent-minded. After a few days, she found out the cause. He told her of Venissa, of her beauty, of her charm, and it was evident to Placidia that Marcus had lost his heart to the British girl.

"Marcus," she said, "you must forget her. I could never wish you to marry other than a girl of your own race. You will be returning to Rome after a few years; imagine this simple, British maiden among our Roman matrons!"

"Mother, she is the daughter of a British chieftain."

"That may be, but compared with the girls of Rome she is a barbarian, doing domestic work, while a true-bred patrician Roman lady does not even fan herself, but calls her slave to do it. She would be ridiculous about her food, and shudder at eating wood-maggots or chickens. Can she read or write? I doubt if she knows the use of rouge, and her eyebrows are probably undarkened."

Marcus made an impatient movement.

"I do not admire that sort of thing in a woman."

"Ah, well, my son, we will not quarrel about her. You will soon forget fair Venissa. I think you said that was her name."

"I shall never forget her," Marcus murmured to himself, "but whether I shall ever win her, I know not. I fear her heart is given to Alaric."

He sat a few moments pondering; then he noticed tears in his mother's eyes.

"What is troubling you, mother, dear?" he asked.

"Troubling me, you ask?" Placidia spoke fretfully. "Have I not many causes of trouble? My little Julia lost; you and your father and, I think, Canace, as far as a child is able, have been ensnared by this new religion, and what disaster that may bring on our family, who can say? Now, to crown all, you speak of wishing to win a British maiden for your wife."

"But, mother, that is no disgrace. Did not Pudens marry Claudia? Was she not respected above many women in our nation?"

"That was different," Placidia answered. "He did not marry her until she had been adopted by the Roman Emperor and her name changed from the British 'Gladys' to the Roman 'Claudia.' All I have to say, Marcus, is that you will go against my wishes, if you persist in this mad idea of yours."

Marcus left his mother with a troubled face, for he hated the thought of grieving her. From their childhood, Felicius had trained his children to be considerate of their mother, and the early teaching bore fruit.

Marcus sought his father and asked: "Father, have you taken any steps about seeking for Julia?"

"Yes, my boy. I have sent two of my men to Glevum; they have made diligent search, but no trace of her can be found. Your mother is bitterly disappointed, as, of course, I am. We must be patient with mother, my son, for it is a sad time for her; she is not pleased to be in Britain; she was thwarted in her desire to be the mother of a Vestal Virgin, always considered a high honour in our nation, and now we have failed to find Julia."

"Father, we are praying about it, and I have the feeling that our prayers will be answered before long."

"Go on praying, Marcus, and ask too that your mother's heart may be opened to receive the good news that means so much to us."

"I do, Father, every day," Marcus answered.

Chapter 23.

Alaric's Commission

ALARIC was sitting with Bernard who lay on his couch looking very feeble. They had been talking long together; now Bernard seemed tired, and they sat in silence. Alaric was watching the old man's face as he lay with closed eyes, and a fear arose in his heart that Bernard's days were numbered. He wondered who would continue his work

Suddenly, there came to his mind some words which Bernard had spoken to him a short time ago. Bernard had been telling him of the young prophet Isaiah and of his response to God's call for him to be the one to carry His warnings and teaching to the nation. His whole life was to be devoted to that service. "Here am I, send me," Isaiah had said, and now the thought came to Alaric: "If God calls me, can I respond thus?"

He shrank from the idea; it came with a shattering blow to all his previous plans and ambitions. To win Venissa, to live a simple, happy home life, maintaining Christian principles both in the home and in the neighbourhood, spreading the Gospel as opportunity offered; but to give his whole life to this work as Bernard had done, travelling here and there? Alaric recoiled from the very suggestion, and yet, had not the Saviour left Heaven with all its glory to come to this poor world, and had not He himself found peace through that great sacrifice which Christ had made?

Alaric bowed his head on his hands and prayed. When he lifted his face from his hands, he found Bernard's eyes fixed on him as if the old preacher knew his thoughts.

Bernard spoke quietly: "My friend, I have it in my mind to ask if you will do for me what I had hoped to do myself. I intended to go shortly back to Gwlad-yr-hav (Cornwall)and see how the young converts are getting on there. I long to be used to build them up in the faith but I am too feeble in body. I know no one whom I can send with such confidence as you. You have been much with me lately, and I have been able to pass on the main teaching of the Holy Scriptures; to you it is entrusted. Will you go forth, relying on the guidance of the Holy Spirit, and visit the villages where I proclaimed the good news?"

Half an hour before, Alaric would have hesitated; now he said quietly: "I would say, as Isaiah said, 'Here am I, send me!' "

"Praise the Lord," Bernard responded.

So, after a few days of preparation, Alaric went forth. Whether this was to be his life work, he could not at the time say; or whether he would be led to give only occasional weeks to this service, still maintaining his home life. At any rate, he felt he could only be absent a limited time while his one near relative, his old father, lived.

It was a sacrifice in which Venissa had her share, for she felt that Alaric would protect and defend her from Leirwg's designs. With Alaric gone, she sought to encourage herself in the Lord, and found her faith strengthened in a special manner as she prayed and sought her Heavenly Father's help. Not that she altogether expected to be kept from suffering, she realised that grace and courage would be given if a testing time came.

The day of the great winter festival arrived, and passed with nothing more than the usual sacrifice of oxen, and the games and feasting. Venissa kept quietly at home during those days. Hulda attended the ceremony and gave her best ox to be sacrificed. Venissa suspected that much gold went to Leirwg at the same time. Hulda was seriously annoyed with Venissa for her refusal to accompany her, but Venissa could not conscientiously be present at the sacrifice with all its ritual, and the sports and games which followed had never attracted her; they were too rough. Even when under her father's protection, she had disliked to witness the horse-play. One game, called the "Badger in the Bag", seemed to her cruel, as did others. In that particular game, a man was tied in a sack, then the others hit him in turn hard blows, until the unfortunate "Badger" could successfully guess who hit him, he had to endure the blows. If he were successful in his guess, the one he named took his place as "Badger" to receive in turn the hearty blows from his fellows.

The spring days came, and all went on as usual. Elfrida was rejoicing in Osmond's presence in her home while he devoted his time largely to the management of the many outdoor servants who worked on the land. Venissa passed her days in caring for Julia, trying to soothe and help her mother, and working with the slaves at the customary tasks both indoors and outdoors. Whenever she had the opportunity, she gathered those who were willing to listen and taught them what she knew of the good news of salvation. Some rejoiced at the tidings and, with true repentance for sin, found their way to the Cross of Christ, there to experience forgiveness and cleansing. Venissa was especially cheered by the way Hubert drank in the message, and she saw by his life that his profession was a reality. He constantly accompanied her to the hut when she went to visit Bernard, and when she herself could not go, he could be trusted to take food to the old man. As Hulda spent most of her time in her own room, Venissa was able to send all that Bernard needed, without arousing any suspicion. Others, too, frequently made their way to the hut; Osmond was often there and all were strengthened in their faith by the teaching they received.

It was a time of peace, and Venissa had almost lost the sense of fear that she used to experience when she thought of Leirwg in former days, and remembered how he had spoken of the dire wrath of the gods which would fall on those who had deserted the old worship as carried out by their forefathers. Leirwg visited Hulda fairly frequently still. He ignored Venissa, for which she was thankful; she only wished to be left in peace.

One day in April, Venissa went to visit Elfrida, taking Julia with her. They spent a happy hour or two there. Elfrida and Osmond both looked so happy, and the atmosphere of the home was so peaceful, Julia and Venissa enjoyed being there. Osmond took Julia to see some puppies and, while Elfrida and Venissa were left alone, Elfrida remarked, after inquiring for Hulda's health, she hoped the time would come when Hulda would shake off Leirwg's power over her.

"It seems to me, Venissa, that Leirwg's authority is waning, so many have now accepted the Gospel. I hope the worship of the false gods will soon be a thing of the past, at any rate, in our neighbourhood. I should think that Bernard could come back to one of our homes and preach openly."

Venissa made no reply. She did not wish to disturb Elfrida's peace of mind, but the girl's old fears had been revived on her way to Elfrida's home, for she had seen a large number of priests, strangers to her, gathered outside Leirwg's dwelling, and she wondered for what reason Leirwg had summoned them. She remembered that it was drawing near the time of the great spring festival, May 1st, and she experienced a sense of foreboding as she saw these men.

Presently, Osmond and Julia came in, Julia laughing and rosy with a puppy in her arms, a little bundle of fluffy wool; the mother, a fine specimen of British sheep dog, followed the child with anxious eyes.

"Venissa, I brought one for you to see. Isn't he a fat tatta? I wish I could keep him" Julia exclaimed.

Venissa duly admired the puppy, and then said: "We must be going, Julia."

Julia reluctantly gave the puppy to Osmond, and the two went home, Osmond escorting them. Julia ran hither and thither picking primroses, shouting with delight when she found some violets and, when the child ran out of hearing, Venissa took the opportunity of telling Osmond of what she had seen.

Osmond shared her fears, but he refrained from expressing them too freely.

"Venissa, dear, we must look up for strength and grace. We are weak in ourselves, and it is only as we are sustained from above that we shall be able to stand firm and not deny our Saviour. It means we should be much in prayer. But all the same it might be that Leirwg means to make the coming festival an impressive one and so needs the support of these extra priests; we must not be too apprehensive."

"I hope that is so but, as you say, we must pray and trust. Were you present last week when Bernard told us that lovely story of those three men in the burning, fiery furnace, and how the Son of God walked in the flames with them and they took no ill?"

"I was there. And surely God is just the same today. The words that David wrote are in my mind: "Yea, though I walk through the valley of the shadow of death, I will fear no evil, for Thou art with me."

Cheered by her cousin's words, Venissa sang softly to herself, as she sat at her embroidery that evening:

"Christ is my Refuge in times of distress;
Christ is my Saviour when enemies press.
Fearless I trust Him to still my alarm;
Safely He holds with His sheltering arm."

Hubert heard her as he came into the room bearing logs for the fire, for the evenings were chilly, and his heart responded although his lips were silent.

"Hubert," Venissa said to him, "if anything should happen to me, I trust you to care for Bernard."

“Oh, my mistress, do not speak of any unpleasant happening. You are not feeling ill, I hope.”

“No, Hubert, but life is uncertain. Praise God, I am ready to die, through the grace and salvation of Jesus Christ.”

Hubert looked at his young mistress wistfully. His devotion to her was great. He had always loved her since the days when, as a very young boy, he had got into trouble through disobedience, and Cynvelin had ordered a severe whipping to be administered. Venissa had begged her father to excuse the lad for once, and Cynvelin had consented to his daughter’s pleadings; now, since the time when Hubert had learnt to love the Saviour through Venissa’s teaching, the lad would have gone through fire and water to save his mistress from distress.

Chapter 24.

Hubert's Search.

A FEW days after this, Venissa went out on an errand of mercy to visit an old woman who was dying. At the time of the evening meal she had not returned. Hubert was on the look out for her, and wondered at her long absence. He fidgeted in and out, talked to Julia who was also restless, saying:

"I wish Venissa would not stay away so long."

At last, Hubert consulted with Amelia, and the two decided to seek Hulda. At the door of Hulda's room, Hubert coughed discreetly, and then gave a slight scratch on the door. Getting no response, Amelia pushed the door ajar. To their dismay, they saw Hulda sitting on the floor with her face buried in her hands.

“Mistress,” Hubert said gently, “Mistress Venissa has not returned; shall I go and seek for her?”

Hulda lifted a face so distorted with grief and horror that the lad shrank back. Her eyes were red with weeping, her face swollen, her hair flung in disorder around her shoulders; her lips drew back over her teeth, and she made a sound like the snarl of an animal. Then, she pulled herself together, evidently making an effort.

“It is no use, Hubert, no use. Your young mistress will never return; she defied the gods, and they will have revenge. Oh, my daughter, my daughter!”

Hulda flung herself full length on the floor, almost beside herself with grief. Hubert turned away, leaving Amelia to deal with her mistress. Amelia quickly got a strong draught, made from a concoction of herbs, and persuaded her mistress to drink it. It had a soothing effect, as Amelia knew it would, and presently Hulda consented to lie on a couch while Amelia sat beside her, gently rubbing her feet and murmuring pacifying words and, before long, Hulda slept.

Meanwhile, Hubert went to little Julia and persuaded her to eat her supper, telling her he would go and look for Venissa; she must go to bed like a good child. Then, calling a young servant to be with Julia, Hubert went off, determined not to return until he had found his young mistress. He went first to the hut, where he knew she had intended paying a visit, and found she had been there quite early in the afternoon, and had left hours before. He stood outside the hut hesitating and, as he stood, he lifted up his heart for guidance. Which way should he go? Just then a man came along, one who had shown a certain amount of interest in the Gospel story, but had not come out boldly for Christ, being still held in fear of the gods and the priests, but he showed a friendly spirit toward those who were Christians; now, seeing Hubert standing in uncertainty, he beckoned to him. Speaking softly, he said: “Are you looking for your mistress? If so, come with me where we can talk without being overheard. I will tell you what I know.”

Hubert followed the man into a copse and, after looking around carefully to see they were not observed, he said: “Your mistress has been taken captive by Leirwg and a band of priests. I saw them seize her this afternoon, when I was working in the fields."

"Oh—h," Hubert said loudly, in horror at the man's statement.

"Hush! keep quiet! You can do nothing. They have taken Mistress Elfrida, her son, and one or two others. I believe they mean to have many more."

"Tell me where they have taken her. I must rescue my mistress."

"Tush, man! You can do nothing. Look out for yourself. It is known that you have forsaken the religion. 'Tis as I always feared it would be; we cannot go against the priests. It only means suffering and perhaps death if we do. Take my advice, and ask Leirwg to forgive your wanderings and tell him you repent."

"Never mind about me," Hubert said. "Tell me if you know where the prisoners are."

"I don't know. I must go, it would not do for me to be seen talking to you."

Hubert caught the man's sleeve, as he seemed about to make off.

"You must tell me which way they went."

"They went north, making, I should think, for Linthorpe. (The village of the waterfall.) Strikes me they are afraid to keep their captives anywhere near here for fear of a rising and a rescue. There, I've said enough. Don't be a fool and run into danger."

So saying, the man made off. Hubert did not hesitate a moment. He must find his mistress; that one idea filled his mind. Of what he could do when he found her he had no thought. He started off at once, and walked until he could no longer find his way in the dark. Then, he climbed a tree for safety from wild beasts and, tying himself to a branch with his belt, he managed to get a little sleep. At dawn, he was off again. He was hungry and thirsty but, so eager was he to find his mistress, he scarcely heeded his own needs. However, he stopped to drink at a sparkling spring of water when he came to it and, later, when reaching a circle of huts, he begged some food. A kindly woman gave him oatcakes and goats' milk and, refreshed, he hurried on. In two days' time, he reached Linthorpe but found, on making inquiries, no one had seen either priests or prisoners.

On consideration, he decided the priests were far too crafty to go straight to any place, but he felt baffled: which way to turn he did not know. Then he remembered God, His Heavenly Father, knew just where the captives were and, asking for guidance, he felt impelled to turn his steps homeward. Constantly praying for directions as he went along, he travelled without adventure; people were kind to him, and several times he received gifts of food. On the second night, he turned away from the beaten track and, not knowing why he did so, he plunged into the forest. It was growing late but not yet quite dark. He was just looking out for a suitable tree in which to spend the night, when he noticed something shining on the ground. He pounced on it, and exclaimed aloud in his astonishment. It was a bangle and he recognised it at once as belonging to his young mistress. Then she had been brought in this direction. This clue gave him fresh courage and he recalled having heard that somewhere in this neighbourhood there was a sacred oak, where the Druids sometimes offered sacrifices. He pushed on and quite soon he came out into an immense clearing. He gasped in astonishment and horror at what he saw. In the centre was a huge wicker cage, roughly shaped like the outline of a human figure; piles of firewood and straw lay around. Hubert knew only too well what it meant; preparations were being made for a great sacrifice on May 1st.

But where were the prisoners? No one seemed to be about. Those who had been at work there had evidently left, returning to their homes for the night. Hubert looked earnestly round in the waning light and then saw a large hut in the shadow of the trees. He crept as quietly as possible to it, not knowing whether a Druidical priest would be acting as sentry, but no one was there. He noted the massive door securely fastened; he walked round to the back where the trees hung over in profusion: there, he discovered a small aperture high up which admitted the necessary air to the hut.

Pausing there, Hubert waited and, as he stood, he heard his mistress's voice.

"Don't cry, darling; Venissa will sing to you." Hubert heard her say.

Then, the sweet comforting words of the hymn so loved by them all rang out clear and true on the evening air.

"Jesus, my Saviour, to Whom should I fly?
Thou art the Rock that is higher than I;
Jesus, my Refuge, my Fortress, my Tower,
Quietly I trust in Thy conquering power."

When Venissa stopped, Hubert started as he heard little Julia's voice.

"Jesus will take care of us, won't He, Venissa?" the child said.

"Yes, darling, He will. We must trust Him."

Hubert drew near and said as loudly as he dared: "Mistress Venissa!"

"Who is it?" Venissa asked.

"It is Hubert, Mistress. What can I do for you? Oh my dear Mistress, is there any way in which I can free you?"

"I fear not, Hubert, we are fastened with chains; but it is good to hear your voice."

Then, some one else spoke, and Hubert recognised the voice as Elfrida's.

"How did you find us, Hubert?"

"I prayed, and God led me," the boy answered simply. "Where is Master Osmond? Is he with you?"

"No. The men are in another hut. We are six women here," Venissa answered. Then, she added: "Oh, Hubert, I do think the best thing you can do for us, is to find Master Alaric. He may think of some plan to help us."

"I will, I will, Mistress. I will seek him at once but, my lady, time is brief. I must start now, and do you pray that I may find him quickly. Is little Mistress Julia with you? I left her safely at home when I started to find you."

"Yes: she was brought here yesterday. I fear my mother gave her up."

Venissa's voice broke in a little sob. She was calm when thinking of her own danger, but the thought of the child suffering broke her down.

"Don't cry, dearest," Elfrida said. "You have been so brave and a cheer to us all."

Hubert, realising that every moment was precious, said: "My lady, I will not delay. I will go at once."

"God bless and prosper your going," several voices spoke at once. "We will pray for your safe journey."

So Hubert sped on his way, too eager to heed fatigue, stopping only when absolutely necessary to get a little food, praying all the time that his steps might be guided.

How great was his joy, after travelling for a day and a night, to fall in with a man who told him that a preacher was staying in his village and, from the description given, Hubert knew it was Alaric.

He hastened in the direction the man pointed out, and soon found Alaric and told his terrible news.

Chapter 25.

Alaric Does His Best.

ALARIC was dumb with intense horror for the moment. Recovering himself, he said: “Thank God, I was so nearly home; somehow I felt impelled, a fortnight ago, to turn my steps in this direction. I have lingered to give the good news in various villages, or I should have been back before this. Now, what shall I do? Let me think.”

Hubert waited in silence until Alaric spoke again.

“I shall return home to our village and raise a band of men to rescue the captives.”

Alaric had his horse, so he hastened on, leaving Hubert to follow on foot. But alas, to Alaric’s great disappointment, not many were willing to aid him. He learnt there were some three hundred Druidical priests in the neighbourhood and, with few exceptions, all the people were in a state of terror.

"It is hopeless," one after another said, "we cannot resist; it would only mean slaughter for us all."

Alaric felt almost driven to despair to think he had wasted two days in trying to raise a band of helpers. One other hope he had, but time was short; he would go to Caer Wyn (Winchester) and seek the aid of Felicius and Marcus. He had no doubt that they would come with a company of soldiers to the rescue.

As soon as Alaric knew his first plan was futile, he hurried off on his strongest horse. He longed to go to the place where the prisoners were, and say words of support to Venissa, but that would have delayed him, so he refused to allow himself this comfort.

On, on, he rode, only pausing to feed and water the animal, or snatch a hasty meal himself. Once he lost his way and wasted valuable time. He seemed occasionally almost dazed with the horror of the situation. Venissa, the young, beautiful girl whom he loved more than life itself, in the grip of those cruel, relentless men, the fateful moment drawing nearer and nearer. Little innocent Julia, Osmond his friend, and others all in imminent peril!

"Oh, God, God, help me to do it," he cried again, and yet again.

The horse responded nobly to his master's mood, but after a while showed signs of fatigue. Alaric hoped to reach some homestead where he could secure another mount, but he was travelling in isolated country, only reaching a few hut circles where the people were peasants and possessed no horses.

At last, he was nearing his goal; he recalled his former journey and reckoned he had about ten more miles to cover when his horse stumbled and fell heavily. Alaric, fortunately, was thrown clear of the animal and, as he scrambled to his feet, he saw the poor beast had rolled over absolutely exhausted. He knew it was useless to expect anything more of the creature, so he hurried forward on foot. Meeting a peasant, he gave him some money to go to the horse and care for it, which the man promised to do.

On, on, on, panting, struggling, Alaric hastened. The blood vessels in his head seemed almost bursting. Mile after mile he covered, now nearly passed clear thinking, just conscious of the necessity of reaching the Roman camp. Once he caught his foot in a treacherous root and fell heavily, cutting his forehead on a sharp stone. He lay stunned for a few moments; then he pulled himself up to a sitting position and found he was crying aloud: "Venissa, Venissa! God save her from the tyrants."

He felt too faint to move, and then suddenly he remembered the story Bernard had told him on the day that he and Marcus had visited the old preacher and found Venissa there. How long ago that happy day seemed! Now he recalled the words Bernard had spoken of the Great High Priest, even Jesus Christ, Who still came to help His needy children in their times of distress.

"Bread to strengthen, wine to cheer and His blessing," he murmured to himself and, even as he said the words, he had a glorious sense of the Presence of that wonderful Saviour Who loved him and Whom he loved. He rose refreshed to go forward and, heedless of his wounded head, he pressed on.

Felicius and Marcus had just finished the duties of the day and were about to turn their steps homeward when, in the waning light, they saw the figure of a man rushing towards them and gesticulating to attract their attention.

"Who is this?" Marcus said, and then exclaimed: "Why it is Alaric! What can be the matter?"

He hurried to meet his friend, and Alaric fell exhausted at his feet.

"What is wrong?" Marcus asked, as he stooped to raise Alaric. "You are spent and wounded."

"Venissa, Venissa," Alaric cried. Then with an effort, for he felt he must tell his tale before he lost consciousness, he continued: "The Druids are preparing to sacrifice Venissa and others on May 1st. They are prisoners and all is ready. Go, go I beseech you, go and save them."

Felicius stooped over the prostrate lad, for Alaric was still sitting on the ground and, calling a soldier, they raised him and carried him into a tent, giving him a strong restorative, while Marcus said:

"Father, we must not delay, give the order, I beg of you, that a band of soldiers may accompany me to the rescue."

The restorative helped Alaric to a measure of recovery and he said: "There are a large number of Druids gathered for the ceremony. You will need at least a hundred men, but do not delay. I am better now and I will go with you."

"No," Felicius said, "you must rest. Marcus will start at once, I will summon my men, and you and I will follow tomorrow. You would only hinder Marcus' speed. You can trust him."

So Alaric consented to rest, feeling that Felicius' words were wise, and, within an hour, he had the satisfaction of knowing a powerful band of well-armed soldiers had started, all eager to suppress the Druids and rescue the prisoners.

Meanwhile, at the first opportunity, Hubert had made his way to Bernard's hut, in order to acquaint him with the terrible calamity which had befallen Venissa, Elfrida, Osmond, Julia, and others, all of whom had been led to Christ through Bernard's teaching.

Bernard was overcome with grief at the lad's story.

"My children! My children in the faith! In the grip of the Druids are they? In the grip of those awful men and I sitting here in safety," he murmured.

Then, rising to his feet, he said: "My boy, I must go to them. I must be there to encourage them to witness to those priests, and stand firm for Christ. I will, by God's grace, proclaim the message of the Cross even to these persecutors; it may be even yet their hearts will be softened, and, if not, I would rather suffer with my children."

"Oh, my master, what shall we do that are left, if you are slain? I feel my young mistress would say I ought not to have told you, if it leads you into danger. Let me beg of you to stay here, you are only one against so many. What can you do?"

"Hubert, if it is God's will, one man can put a thousand to flight by His power, or He can send His hosts to fight for us; if not, why should

I be shielded while others suffer? Do not hinder me, my son, rather aid me with your young, strong arm to do the rough, long walk."

Hubert saw it was useless to plead, so he said: "I pray you, master, take some of this broth which I have brought to strengthen you; and here are jellied eels which Amelia always says are very nourishing. And I have brought also some calves-foot jelly; the strength of the calf enters into you as you take it."

Bernard felt the wisdom of Hubert's advice. He would need physical strength for the journey, so he ate the food, insisting that Hubert shared the meal; then, he knelt in prayer, asking for guidance, for grace to witness or suffer, both for himself and for the captives; and for Hubert that God would keep him in the upward path and make him a bold, brave soldier of the Cross. Hubert never forgot that prayer as long as he lived; the scene was burnt into his memory, the earnestness of the old teacher, the yearning tones, the loving look, as they rose from their knees, stirred the young man to the depths of his being.

It was late in the evening when Bernard, at last, reached the sacred grove, and the priests were absent. That was what Bernard had hoped for as it gave him the opportunity of going to each hut and giving a message to the prisoners. When he spoke at the barred grating and his voice was recognised, there were mingled exclamations of joy and dismay. Joy at hearing their dear leader's tones once again, dismay, that he was there in that perilous spot. However, one suggested that Bernard could make his escape before the priests came in the morning, so they settled down to listen to him. It was a time of solemnity and yet joy, for the One Who suffers with His suffering children drew near as they prayed and communed together.

Then, they sang their hymn and, in the darkness of the night, there rang out the triumphant words:

"What can we add to the fullness of praise?
Forms of Thine earth-dust, Thy glory we raise.
Peace Thou hast purchased for souls dead before Thee,
Christ, we exalt Thy Name! God, we adore Thee!"

When Bernard visited the men's hut, Osmond and the others begged him to leave before dawn, but the old man refused.

"I want, if possible, to give my testimony to the priests. Many of them have never heard of the Saviour."

The first to arrive at the clearing in the morning was Leirwg, attended by one priest only. He stared in amazement when he saw Bernard.

"The man is mad," Leirwg said to his companion. "He is deliberately putting himself in our power.''

If Leirwg expected Bernard to rush away and seek a hiding place at his approach, he was mistaken. Bernard calmly came to meet the priests. Lifting his hands, he said: " Leirwg, I have a message for you from God your Creator. Beware! you are defying Him; you are persecuting His children. Judgement will fall upon you. God is not mocked, whatever a man sows, that shall he also reap. God is looking down now on you, He beholds all that you do; more than that, He knows your thoughts."

Then, Bernard's voice broke with emotion as he suddenly recalled Christ's love for His enemies and His cry: "Father, forgive them: they know not what they do."

The old preacher cried: "Leirwg, there is forgiveness even for you. I bring you not only a message of warning, but also one of love and light. God grant you repentance. May His Light shine into your heart, revealing the evil. Alas, alas! You and your fellow priests have darkened minds; you love darkness rather than light, because your deeds are evil. Satan has enslaved you, but there is One Who can break the chains and set you free. It is you who are the captive, bound in darkness. These men and women, whom you think are your prisoners, are the free ones of God. You cannot bind their spirits; you may do your worst to their bodies, but their souls will take their flight to the Heavenly abode where Christ is and where all is light and love."

Leirwg stood as if spellbound. Again, he heard those words which Venissa had spoken and which he could never quite banish from his mind: "Men love darkness rather than light, because their deeds are evil."

A group of priests had arrived by this time and Leirwg, with a howl of rage, shook himself free from the thought surging in his mind of the contrast between darkness and light and, shouting to his subordinates to assist him, he rushed on Bernard and together they hustled him off, roughly handling him, and thrust him inside the men's hut.

Chapter 26.

The Great Spring Festival.

THE first day of May dawned, a delightful, soft, pearly-grey morning. A twitter of birds in the bushes greeted the morn, soon to be followed by a glorious burst of song from hundreds of throats; the cuckoo called happily as the sun rose shining in its strength.

The prisoners in the huts in the Druids' sacred grove had spent most of the night in prayer, and in encouraging one another. Only little Julia slept, and thankful were the others that she did. They had carefully kept the knowledge from her that this was the night before the festival.

Leirwg and the other priests were up early, prostrating themselves before the rising sun, taking it as an omen of the sun god's approval of the proposed sacrifice that no cloud dimmed the sky. Leirwg, as Arch-Druid, had put on his official robes of scarlet and gold brocade, while the other priests were all in spotless white. More often than not, the great sacrifice was made at dawn but, giving no reason for his decision, Leirwg decreed that it was to be at sunset. Perhaps his intensely cruel nature desired to gloat all day over the helpless condition of the victims. He intended, too, to make it as impressive as possible to the onlookers by having a day of chants, invocations and much ritual.

Two beautiful white oxen were led to the place of slaughter; the prisoners were brought forth from the huts and arranged in rows.

Leirwg and many others looked with amazement at the calm faces of these men and women, some young, some old, who were in their power. They marvelled greatly, for they were strangers to the peace that God gives in times of trial.

Many speeches were made, the priests seeking to rouse to enthusiasm the great crowd of people that stood round, but in vain; sullen faces were seen on every side. Leirwg had been wise in bringing such a number of priests to his aid; it was doubtful if the fear of the gods alone would have been sufficient to have kept back the people from attempting a rescue.

About mid-day, when the sun was at its zenith, the oxen were sacrificed. Then, when the flames died down, Leirwg addressed the prisoners. He said that in his desire for mercy he would give them each one chance more to save his or her own life. He must make one exception to this, and that was Osmond, a man so degraded that, after having enjoyed the privileges of priesthood, he had deliberately forsaken the religion of his forefathers and disgraced the sacred order of Druids. He could only be condemned to death; there was no pardon for him, not even if he repented.

The fact was that Osmond knew too many of their secrets, knew too much about their deceitful practices to be allowed to live. They must silence him by death.

Elfrida hid her face in her hands, as she heard the priest proceed to curse her son; to condemn him to everlasting torment; to say all manner of evil things about him, but Osmond's countenance shone with a light not born of earth.

Leirwg continued: "We are willing to spare the lives of those who repent of their wrong, and promise to come back to the worship of the gods, yet such a defection from the path of right-doing must be punished. Instead of death by fire, each man and woman who recants will become the property henceforth of the principal priests, to be treated according to the will of their owners."

Leirwg paused. A low groan broke from the crowd, for all realised that such a punishment was worse than death. To be a slave for life was a sentence of horrible cruelty.

Then, Leirwg spoke to each one individually. One after the other replied to his question calmly, refusing to deny the Saviour Who had redeemed them. Before Venissa, Leirwg lingered, and spoke with extra severity.

"Did I not tell you, Venissa, that disaster would follow your defiance of the gods? You richly deserve punishment, but now, for the last time, I ask you, will you come back to the worship of the gods, whom as a child, you were taught to honour?"

"They are no gods," Venissa answered. "I worship and belong to the one true God. You can destroy my body, but you cannot touch my spirit. That will go to my Heavenly Father. In His Home are many mansions and one is prepared for me. I believe that, because my Saviour took my place on Calvary, bearing the punishment I deserved, I am forgiven."

Venissa could say no more, for the priests positively howled with rage. Instead of the girl's beauty, innocence and fearlessness stirring pity in their hearts, it brought forth diabolical hate. Leirwg's eyes gleamed with a wicked loathing. He lost his usual self-control and, lifting his hand, he struck Venissa a heavy blow on her cheek.

Again, a low, ominous growl broke from the onlookers, while Elfrida said clearly: "Venissa, remember our Saviour. He was smitten for us."

"I do, and I am comforted," Venissa replied.

The long weary day dragged on. All eyes watched the sun going slowly down in the west. Little Julia mercifully fainted, unable to bear any more; she had had no food for twenty-four hours, and the awful strain was too much for her; she sank unconscious on the grass, and Venissa and Elfrida both murmured: "Thank God." Venissa longed to lift the child in her arms, but she was bound with chains, and could not move or free her arms.

"It will soon be over, dear," Elfrida whispered to Venissa, and Osmond repeated in a loud, clear voice words he had only recently learnt from Bernard: "What are these which are arrayed in white robes? And whence came they? These are they which have come out of great tribulation, and have washed their robes, and made them white in the blood of the Lamb. Therefore are they before the throne of God, and serve Him day and night in His temple: and he that sitteth on the throne shall dwell among them. They shall hunger no more, neither thirst any more; neither shall the sun light on them, nor any heat." He repeated the last words again, thinking of the fire which they were about to experience, "Nor any heat."

Leirwg commanded him to be quiet but he refused to be silenced, so the priests began to chant loudly. Some of them were weary of waiting, and felt annoyed with Leirwg that the sacrifice had been delayed so long. Beginning to be conscious of the annoyance of his subordinates, Leirwg gave the order that the prisoners were to be placed in the cage and the final arrangement of the firewood made. But before he had finished his sentence, there came a sudden sound; everybody heard it. A silence fell on all. They well knew what the noise was. As the Romans rode into battle, they always clanged their scabbards against their shields, producing a penetrating din. This was the sound that came on the evening air, bringing pallor to the cheeks of the priests, and a throb of relief to the hearts of the captives and most of the people standing round.

Leirwg and his confederates looked wildly round on every side for an avenue of escape but, as one man, the people crowded round, blocking every pathway. It was easy to see on whose side the sympathy of the crowd was placed. It was only a few moments from the time when the first sound had reached the clearing to the minute when the people hastily made room for a hundred Roman soldiers, led by Marcus, galloping into the centre of the scene. Their swords were uplifted; all was confusion; the priests sought to escape, but for the majority it was a vain effort. The people sided with the Romans and dire punishment fell on the men who only a short time before were cruelly and deliberately planning the suffering of the helpless Christians; but God was for them and, when the testing time was over, His deliverance came.

Marcus left the battle to his men and hastened himself to release the captives. Venissa, first of all, and then the others, leading them quickly out of the fray to a quiet spot in the forest.

"Wait here," he said, "I will be back shortly and will take you to your homes."

He had picked up the unconscious form of Julia and, placing her in Venissa's arms, he said: "Care for this little maiden."

Venissa and Elfrida chafed the child's hands, loosening the rope which was cutting into the little wrists. Osmond quickly noticed a streamlet near and brought water to bathe her face. Presently, with a convulsive shudder, Julia opened her eyes. She hid her face on Venissa's shoulder, sobbing.

It was some ten minutes before Venissa could calm the child, assuring her they were all going home, and there was no more danger.

"God has delivered us, Julia. We are quite safe now. Do not cry, my pet, no one is going to hurt you," Venissa said over and over again until at last the child's sobs ceased, but she was still weary and half famished for food.

As soon as possible, Marcus returned to the little group and, placing the women on horses, some of the soldiers leading them, all returned to their homes, almost too dazed to take in what had happened.

"Praise God," was heard on every side from many lips.

Marcus took Julia in his arms carrying her gently, while Osmond helped Bernard along.

Presently, Marcus asked, as he walked by Venissa's horse: "Is she your little sister?"

"She is my adopted sister, but we do not know really who she is. She was brought to us a little captive and my father and mother adopted her. She is very precious to me now."

Marcus exclaimed under his breath, then spoke quietly.

"How long ago was this? Do you know her name?"

Julia then unexpectedly spoke up for herself. "My name is Julia," she said.

While Venissa said: "I think it must be about three or four years ago."

"Then, I believe she is my little sister," Marcus said with trembling voice. "We were stationed at Glevum (Gloucester) when our baby sister was only three years old and she was lost. Oh, how thankful my parents will be to you for all your care of her. Strange, that I did not recognise her, but three years makes a difference to such a tiny child."

"You will perhaps see that she is the same when her face regains its colour and the tear stains washed away. She does not look her pretty self at all just now. It is wonderful to think she is your sister, but, oh, I do not want to lose her!" Venissa said. Marcus thought of a way whereby Venissa need not lose her little adopted sister, but he refrained from saying anything just then. For a moment, hope filled his heart, but then he remembered Alaric. He was afraid that Venissa's life-long friend was also her lover. He checked the words that rose to his lips and, instead, spoke to Julia.

"Darling little girl, I am your brother, Marcus. I can take you to your own Mother and Father, and to your sisters, Canace and Flora."

If he had expected Julia to express pleasure, he was disappointed. Instead, she burst into tears, crying: "No, no. I want to stay with 'Nissa. Go away, nasty man."

She struggled to get out of Marcus' arms, and he was obliged to pass her over to Venissa.

"You must not feel grieved," Venissa said. "She has suffered so much this last fortnight, and she has had no food since yesterday. She is easily frightened today. We must go slowly and let her get accustomed to the idea of change. There, darling, don't cry. Your big, kind brother won't take you away, if you don't want to go, I am sure."

"No, no, never. I don't want to go, never."

Julia was most emphatic in her desire.

Marcus was horrified to find that all the captives were more or less faint for want of food, and thankful to arrive at Venissa's home. Great was the outcry from Venissa's servants when she rode into the courtyard. One or two shrank away in fear.

"Our lady's ghost," they cried.

But the more sensible came forward with exclamations of joy. Amelia rushed to meet her with tears running down her face, holding out her arms in welcome, saying over and over again: "Then, the Lord has protected you," while Hubert seemed too overcome to make any remark; his features worked with emotion, and he had difficulty in restraining his tears.

They would have gone on exclaiming and rejoicing endlessly, had not Marcus, seeing that Venissa swayed on her horse and looked ready to faint, said: "Your lady needs food and rest at once. Please attend to your duties."

Venissa, too, making an effort to combat the faintness that was threatening her, said: "Hubert, take the horses, and you," turning to an elderly slave, "see that the soldiers are fed. Amelia, fetch your mistress."

"I want to introduce you, sir, to my mother," she continued, speaking to her deliverer.

So, together they entered the house, Marcus saying: "Please call me Marcus, as you did when we met before, and will you not have some food without delay? I can wait for an introduction to your mother."

Amelia now appeared with jugs of milk, of which Venissa and Julia drank eagerly.

"What is all this disturbance about?" a fretful voice was heard in the corridor. "Who is it that you have admitted, Amelia?"

"Mother! Mother! I am safe, quite safe now. The Roman soldiers came and the Druids have been punished. God has delivered us," Venissa cried.

Hulda tottered, and almost fell.

"My daughter! My daughter! I can scarce believe my eyes. Is it really true that your God has been strong enough to help; stronger than the sun-god?"

"Yes, mother. I will tell you all about it later. This is Marcus who led the soldiers to our rescue."

Hulda seemed to regain something of her former practical good sense and hospitable manner. Turning to Marcus, she said: "I thank you, sir, for your good service to my daughter. I cannot say much, for I can scarcely realise what has happened. I was prostrate with terror and grief, and I cannot recover in a moment."

"There is no need to thank me, lady. Rather, may I ask that your daughter and the little one may have the food they need without delay.?"

Several of the slaves had been bustling round, and Amelia announced that a meal was ready and, after Venissa and Julia had had a quick wash, they gathered round the trestle-boards and had supper.

Venissa said to Marcus when she had a quiet opportunity, speaking in an undertone: "Do not mention to my mother that Julia is your little sister until the child has gone to bed. We must not let her dwell on that thought tonight."

Julia nearly fell asleep with a piece of bread and honey in her hand, so Amelia carried her off.

Then Venissa told her mother of Marcus' relationship to the child.

Hulda was cautious. She asked: "Are you sure of this? Can you give me a description of the garments she wore when you lost her?"

"My mother could do that better than I can," Marcus replied. Then a thought occurred to him.

"I do remember that she wore a golden bangle engraved with a pattern which was uncommon. I can draw it for you."

He took from an inner pocket a small wax tablet and a stylus, and proceeded to inscribe on the tablet a pattern. He passed it to Venissa who took it eagerly and said: "Yes, that is the pattern of Julia's bangle."

“Then, no doubt, she belongs to you,” Hulda said, and then went to fetch the bangle for Marcus’ inspection. They all felt that it was proved that Julia was the lost child of Felicius and Placidia.

Venissa and her mother sat together that night and talked.

Hulda could hardly believe that she need no longer dread Leirwg and his threats. She was still timid and finally said: “I must wait and see. We are free from the priests, but will the gods intervene and punish us?”

“You need have no fear, mother, dear. They are false gods without power, which Leirwg wished us to worship. The one true God has saved us from the tyrants’ grip, and we are free to serve Him.”

“I only hope that is so, my child. Oh, it is wonderful to feel I have you home again, I have suffered such agonies lately. I can scarcely believe this is true.”

Chapter 27.

Venissa Learns To Read

MARCUS stayed some days in Hulda's home. There was a good deal of clearing up to do. The sacred grove was destroyed and the leading men of the neighbourhood summoned to a council. Felicius and Alaric had now arrived, and Felicius spoke with all the authority of the Roman army behind him. He told them plainly that no longer must the old hideous worship be carried on. If he expected opposition, he was agreeably surprised. The Gospel had found an entrance into the hearts of many; some had long secretly hated the tyranny of the priests, while others were quite indifferent to religion at all.

Not a priest was to be seen in the district. Some sixty or seventy had lost their lives in the fight; the others, Leirwg among them, had disappeared. Alaric was appointed deputy to see that Felicius' commands were carried out, and to Bernard was committed the charge of the public worship. Great was the rejoicing, for Leirwg and the other priests had, with their tyrannical rule, unwittingly prepared the people for a new regime. Those who had become Christians in the neighbourhood had shown by their behaviour something of the beauty and love of God, by which means the soil in many hearts had been prepared for the sowing of the good seed.

Marcus was delighted at the opportunity afforded of getting to know Venissa better, and he hoped that their time together would result in Venissa learning to love him. Venissa was shy with him at first, thinking that he, being a Roman, would be accustomed to greater luxuries than the British home afforded and that he would think of her as belonging to an inferior race. But Marcus' training as a soldier made him indifferent to the soft things of life; besides which, both as a man and a Christian, he had no desire to be pampered. And as for thinking Venissa inferior, he considered her in most ways vastly superior to the painted, idle, supercilious women with whom his mother associated.

The great bond between them was their desire to know more of the things concerning the kingdom of God. Together, they often went to Elfrida's home where Bernard was now staying, and they joined with others in hearing the Scriptures read and expounded by the old preacher. Venissa, seeing Marcus' interest in the parchment rolls which Bernard possessed, began to feel a greater respect for the arts of reading and writing.

One morning, she said to Marcus: "I wish I could read and write. You know, as a nation we have always been led to understand that reading was only necessary for people with poor memories. We have prided ourselves on being able to keep in mind long accounts of history, verse, or anything we wished to remember. Now, I begin to long to be able to read the Holy Scriptures for myself."

"Venissa," Marcus replied, "let me teach you to read. It will be a joy for me to do so."

Venissa flushed with pleasure, not only at the thought of learning to read, but also that Marcus should be her teacher, and also that, having learned to read, she would not feel such a gulf between herself and Marcus and his father. She humbly thought much of the superiority of the conquering race, of whom she had heard many wonderful stories, not the least being that many of the women were taught to read and write. Venissa, of course, knew her cousin Osmond could read, having learnt at his university [11], but that ordinary men and women should do likewise had till now seemed unnecessary.

The first difficulty that presented itself was that Marcus had no parchment or vellum with him, no writing material in fact, save the small wax tablet and stylus which he carried in his pocket. Venissa's quick wit solved the problem. She exclaimed: "Let us go to the sand heap and make the letters in the sand."

There was a large heap of silver sand in the compound, kept for cleansing purposes, so there they went every day, and Marcus was charmed with the rapid progress of his pupil. It was not to be wondered at that the lessons were sometimes put on one side and forgotten in the pleasure of conversation, as Marcus told Venissa many things about Rome, the meetings in the catacombs, his mother, and his little sisters, while Venissa had her story to tell, of her childish days, of her dear, good father and his sad death.

Occasionally, Venissa persuaded Julia to join them, but not often, for Julia wanted to keep away from Marcus as much as possible, saying: "I don't want that big soldier man to carry me off, and I don't want to know anything about *Alpha, Beta, Gamma.*"

Poor child, her former experiences of being carried off had made her wary, so now she kept with Hulda, or Amelia, only longing for the time when Marcus should depart, and she would have her dear Venissa to herself again.

Alaric came along sometimes and watched the progress of learning with gloomy eyes. It was evident, only too sadly evident, to him that there was a sparkle in Venissa's eyes, a light on her face that he had

[11] In Caesar's time the Druids were using Greek characters in their letters.

never been able to bring there. It was torture to him to see it, so he kept away mostly and spent a good deal of his time in learning to read also, Bernard being his teacher. Part of every day was given to visiting the converts, and he also helped Bernard in the public worship which was now carried on in security and peace.

At last, the time came when Felicius felt that his work and that of his son's was done. He reminded Marcus that their duties at Caer Wyn (Winchester) must not be neglected. Marcus sighed, and his father inquired what was troubling him.

"You know, father, I long to win Venissa, but two things hold me back. First, I feel sure Alaric loves her, and have I the right to want to marry her? Then, my mother objects to a British girl."

Felicius pondered for a while; at last, he said: "Well, my boy, I think a little waiting will do no harm to either of you. If this is the will of our Heavenly Father, He will bring it to pass. Seek for patience. It may be when your mother knows of Venissa's kindness to our little Julia, her heart will be softened towards Venissa. For myself, my son, I could wish no better bride for you; she is a fair jewel. You have my best wishes. Perhaps you are mistaken about our friend Alaric."

When Felicius had first heard from his son on his arrival that Julia had been found he could scarcely believe his ears. That the child should have found a home where she was kindly treated nearly broke the father down.

"My son," he said in a voice choked with emotion, "I am ashamed of my unbelief; although I prayed daily for my little daughter, I harboured fears that she was a slave somewhere, maybe being trained to evil ways. Indeed, God has been better to me than all my greatest hopes. Take me to the child."

Felicius could not thank Hulda and Venissa enough for all they had done, and he would have loved to clasp Julia with a fatherly embrace, but the poor child had suffered so much, both as baby of three and now again in her seventh year, that she distrusted every one, save a few well-known friends. She clung to Venissa and was in a state of terror if Marcus or Felicius touched her. There was even a danger of brain fever; at night she would sometimes awake screaming: "Don't let Leirwg get me."

It took all Venissa's skill and tenderness to soothe her and, as for letting her go to her mother when Felicius and Marcus departed, every one saw it was impossible.

"We must give her time to forget all she has suffered, poor child," her father said.

Then Venissa made a suggestion.

"Could you not bring your wife and little daughters here, sir? If they stayed with us for a time, Julia would learn to love them. I know I must part with her, although I dread doing so; she has been such a joy to me in these dark days of my life."

Felicius thanked her for her invitation and agreed it would be the best plan.

Then, he said: "I hope you will never again pass through such a time of trial. You have come through triumphantly and proved that God's grace was sufficient, did you not?"

"Yes, indeed. It was wonderful at times in that dark, damp hut in the forest; it seemed lit with the glory of God. The priests got extremely angry at our singing. We sang real songs of praise although, now and again, we felt the shrinking from the prospect of pain. But when the terrible day came, we were all upheld with a power from on high. As I looked at Elfrida, and saw her calm and even shining face, knowing how timid she had formerly been, I realised for myself the reality of God's love and power. Looking back on the experience now, it seems well worthwhile to have suffered, in order to learn what God can do for one."

"I believe that is probably always so," Felicius answered, "that our Father in Heaven makes up to his suffering saints for their pain, in a way that the worldling can not understand."

Chapter 28.

Alaric's Proposal.

WHEN Felicius and Marcus arrived at Caer Wyn and told their news, there was great excitement in the villa. Placidia seemed unable to express her joy in words. Canace's sensitive face flushed with colour; she remembered her little sister distinctly, and Flora, although she had almost forgotten Julia, was delighted at the thought of a playfellow. She said naively: " I shall not require a little slave girl now. I shall have Julia."

"She won't be your slave, Flora; you will have to be a kind, big sister to her, and make her happy," Marcus said.

"But why have you not brought her here?" Placidia naturally inquired. "I grudge every day those people keep her."

"Dearest, you must understand the little one has suffered great terror," Felicius began to explain. Placidia interrupted: "I thought you said they were kind to her."

"Yes, Venissa, of whom Marcus has told you, had been kindness itself to our child, but the Druidical priests had taken our little one captive. You remember we went to suppress them. Marcus rescued Julia, Venissa, and others, just in the nick of time. Enough about that; the point is this, we could not separate Julia from her friends; she is terrified of others, especially men, so the only thing we can do is to accept the kind invitation sent to you and the girls. If you, Canace and Flora go there to stay, Julia will learn to love you and be willing to come home."

"Suppose she never learns to love us! I dare say that Venissa girl will try to poison her mind against us. I never trust these British barbarians."

"Mother!" Marcus exclaimed.

"Hush! my boy," Felicius intervened. Turning to his wife, he said: "My dear, Venissa is no barbarian. She is the daughter of a British chief and every inch a gentlewoman; moreover, we owe her a debt of gratitude beyond my power of telling. Just think what Julia's fate would have been, had not Venissa persuaded her father to buy Julia and, in the kindness of her heart, she has treated the child as a little sister."

"Mother, it will be better for you not to go there, unless you are going to treat Venissa as an equal," Marcus said sturdily.

Placidia's eyes flashed.

"Marcus, do you think I do not know how to behave as a guest? As to whether Venissa is worthy of our friendship, I shall judge for myself. Felicius, I hope you discovered who stole the child and had them well punished."

"No; I was so delighted at having found her, I gave that no thought," Felicius answered.

"Just like you: so easy," Placidia answered.

She lay back on her couch and closed her eyes, intimating that the conversation was closed. Marcus went out of the room. Canace followed him and, slipping her arm into his, said: “Marcus, I know I shall love Venissa, both because you and father think highly of her, and because she had been so good to our Julia.”

“Thank you, dear,” Marcus replied with a happy smile, “I am sure you will love her and you must teach Flora to do the same.”

“I think it will be best to let Flora find out how nice Venissa is for herself. You know, Marcus, she is so naughty that if I tell her to do a thing, she does just the opposite to tease me.” Marcus laughed.

“She is a monkey. You are wiser than I am, Canace. But, dear, I do want you all to love Venissa. It will mean a lot to me, if you do.”

Marcus was disappointed when he found his father did not mean him to accompany Placidia, Canace and Flora, to pay their visit to Hulda and Venissa.

“We cannot both be absent from Caer Wyn again so soon after our return, and I wish to escort your mother there myself. I shall not remain with them, but return here at once. Possibly, you will be able to fetch them in a few weeks’ time.”

Felicius knew his son was disappointed, but he felt it wiser to let Placidia make acquaintance with Venissa without Marcus.

Marcus replied: “Very well, sir. I shall look forward to going later, with your permission.”

Marcus was too well-trained, both as a son and a soldier, to demur at his father’s wishes and commands.

Placidia, in spite of her remarks, made, possibly, partly to tease her son, was feeling a sensation of warm gratitude to Venissa for her care of Julia. Contrary as Placidia often was, yet she was tender-hearted towards her babies. As the children grew older, she apparently took less interest in them, and, as Julia had been just at the most interesting age of babyhood, full of innocent prattle and loving little ways when Placidia lost her, the mother had never ceased to mourn for her child, especially as her fate had been so uncertain.

Now, Placidia was eager to be off, and Felicius, as soon as he could arrange to leave his post, was as keen as his wife to start. Felicius thoughtfully sent a messenger ahead to tell Venissa to expect them.

It was with mixed feelings that Venissa awaited the arrival of her guests. Thankful she was that her mother, although very frail still, was more normal in mind. Each day brought a measure of improvement in Hulda's condition: she even consented to listen to Venissa's repetition of a portion of Scripture. The fact that those who loved God had been delivered from their enemies had made a great impression on Hulda. Hesitatingly, she would say: "It does seem as though your God must be a Reality and stronger than the old gods we worshipped."

Then, again, fears would triumph for a time and she would shiver with apprehension, looking round her with haunted eyes.

"But suppose, if, after all, the gods hear me and are angry!" she would say.

It needed all Venissa's calm confidence to bring any conviction to her poor tempest-tossed mother, to give her any assurance of safety. Yet, Venissa felt that slowly but surely the Light was beginning to dawn in Hulda's heart. It was a good thing that visitors were expected, for it gave Hulda something in which to be interested and kept her from thinking too much of the past.

Julia, too, was pleased to hear that a little girl was coming to see her. Nothing was said to the child of the probable change in her life. All her friends agreed that, for a time, until Julia's mind had recovered from the shock she had received, it would be better not to discuss her future. Julia seemed to have forgotten or, at any rate, to have ceased to think seriously of Felicius's claim on her. Happier days seemed to have dawned for the household.

Elfrida, Bernard and Osmond were frequent visitors, but Venissa wondered why Alaric was not coming in and out as formerly. Then she heard that Alaric's father was dying, so she concluded that was the reason. Osmond spent a good deal of time with Alaric, helping to care for the old man, and guessing at Alaric's secret, Osmond's sympathy was helpful to Alaric's sad heart.

One day, Julia was playing happily in the courtyard when Venissa sought her. The child ran to meet her and, to Venissa's surprise, said: "Venissa, don't let that man who wanted me to call him 'father' come here again, nor that Marcus soldier man, I don't want them."

"Dear, have you forgotten how kind they were to us, how Marcus saved us on that dreadful day?"

Venissa, in her desire to reconcile Julia to the thought of her relations, forgot for the moment her intention not to remind the child of the terrible experience through which she passed. Julia, however, was not so upset as Venissa feared she might be. Childlike, she was already forgetting the trial and regaining balance of mind.

Julia shrugged her shoulders.

"I don't care. I love you and Alaric. Venissa, I'll tell you a big secret. When I am grown up, I am going to marry Alaric; then you will be an old, old woman and we will take care of you."

Venissa's laugh rang out merrily. Hulda sitting in the house heard it with pleasure; it even brought a smile to her faded cheek, it seemed like an echo from the old happy days. For long weeks, no laugh had been heard in that sad home.

"I shan't be so very old, darling, when you are grown up," Venissa said.

Julia looked doubtful; then, catching sight of some one coming, she exclaimed joyfully: "Here comes Alaric. I'll tell him my plan."

She darted off so swiftly that she failed to hear Venissa's, "Don't, Julia, you must not."

The child lifted a gleeful face to meet Alaric's grave one. "Alaric, I've got a lovely plan. I was just telling Venissa, I am going to marry you when I'm big, and then we will take care of dear 'Nissa, cause we both love her, don't we?"

"Yes, indeed we do."

Venissa had joined them now and, seeing Alaric's serious expression, she sent Julia into the house and then asked: "How is your father, Alaric?"

"He passed away at dawn, Venissa, and I believe the Light had shone into his heart."

"Poor Alaric. The home will be lonely for you now. I am so sorry."

Alaric's eyes shone with a tender light, as he looked into the fair face lifted to his, with a sweet indication of sympathy.

"Dear, you heard what little Julia said. You know, don't you, that I want you to say what she said, 'Alaric, I am going to marry you?' I did not mean to speak today, coming from the death-bed of my father, but my heart is sore, and I want the comfort of your love."

Venissa gave a little cry of pain.

"Oh, Alaric! I have always loved you, of course I do, but—but—I have always thought of you as my big brother, my dear brother."

She put her hands over her face and caught her breath in a sob; she could not bear to add to Alaric's sorrow.

There was a moment of silence; then, Venissa lifted her face and said bravely: "Alaric, I will marry you. I won't be selfish and disappoint you. You have always been so good to me and you nearly killed yourself, Felicius told me, in the effort you made to reach him in time for my rescue."

Alaric smiled a wan, piteous smile.

"My little Venissa, you do not understand a man's love. I love you more than I love myself. I could not accept such a sacrifice from you. Your happiness is more to me than my own. Lift your eyes to mine, darling, and tell me is there anyone else?"

A rosy blush mounted slowly in Venissa's face, colouring her cheeks, her neck and her shoulders.

"Tell me dearest, is it Marcus?" said Alaric, quickly reading the tell-tale blushes.

Venissa again hid her face and said not a word. Alaric heard a sob and, putting his arm around her, he said: " Dearest, I do not think I am betraying our friend. He does care for you, and, when he comes, take your happiness. It will be enough for me to know you are happy. Good-bye, good-bye. You will always be the fairest of the fair to me. Lift your face and smile once again at me, little one, that I may carry it in my heart for the rest of my life, the vision of your face in sunshine."

Venissa made an effort and did as she was bid. Alaric with a choked sob turned away.

Venissa hurried into her bedroom. She could not bear to meet anyone just then, she felt shaken and sorrowful.

"Poor, poor Alaric," she murmured. "Oh how selfish and wicked I am! I have taken from him love, friendship, sacrifice, and, now, I have nothing to give him in exchange. Oh! why could we not go on as formerly?"

She would much rather have remained in solitude but her mother came to the door.

"Venissa, why has Alaric gone away so quickly? I wanted to inquire for his father."

"His father died at dawn, mother," Venissa replied.

"Is that the reason for your tears, dear?"

Venissa flushed. She wished she could have answered "yes." But it would have been untrue, so she hung her head and whispered "No."

Hulda looked at her keenly and then said: "Venissa, at one time had Alaric asked your hand in marriage, I should have withheld my consent, although I know your father wished it, but Leirwg was against it and I, as you know, feared to disobey him. Now, however, I begin to feel a sense of freedom and as though I can once again act according to my own judgement, and I wish if Alaric should ask you, that you should accept this offer."

"Mother, Alaric has asked me to marry him and I refused him this morning."

"What nonsense is this? You do not know what is good for you. I am now going to visit Alaric to offer my sympathy on his loss and shall, if opportunity offers, tell him that I wish you to become his wife."

"Mother, I do not feel I love him enough."

"Love will grow, child. You do not dislike him?"

"No, no certainly not."

"We'll argue no more. Dear, dear! What are maidens coming to, I don't know I am sure. When I was young, I was given in marriage as my parents wished, and their judgement was not at fault. No one could have had a better husband than mine. I shall make Alaric happy today. He needs comfort now."

So saying, Hulda departed, intent on carrying out her wishes.

Calling Amelia to attend her, she made her way to Alaric's home and, after condoling with him on his loss, she told her desire.

To her amazement, Alaric shook his head sadly.

"No, dear lady, I cannot compel Venissa. I want her to be happy in her own way. There must be suffering; better for it to be mine than Venissa's. Better one than two."

"Two! To whom do you refer," Hulda asked.

Alaric would not satisfy Hulda's curiosity on that point, and, completely mystified, she returned to her home.

It was not until some days afterwards that light on the matter dawned in her mind. When Felicius, Placidia, Canace and Flora arrived, Hulda noticed a look of disappointment on her daughter's face, as she saw that Marcus was not included in the family group. Hulda thought to herself: "Can it be that Venissa has lost her heart to that young Roman soldier? That is the result of all these lessons in reading and writing."

Felicius left next day, leaving his wife and daughters but, before he left, he sought an interview with Hulda in seclusion.

He then told her of his son's desire, and asked whether she would be willing to give her consent.

Hulda sighed at the thought of losing her daughter and pondered. Then she asked: "Sir, may I inquire whether your wife is favourable to this? I should not like my daughter to be disdained by her mother-in-law. Venissa is as well born as any maiden in Britain, but she is British; your son belongs to our conquerors."

"Lady, I admit that my wife has a prejudice against our son marrying a girl of another nation than his own, but she said to me this morning, 'I can never repay the kindness shown to my little Julia in this household and I feel I shall love Venissa both for that and for her own sake. She will grace any home, whether in Britain or Rome.' "

Hulda was naturally pleased at the compliment paid her daughter, but she refused to express a definite opinion. She had so long leaned on others for advice and direction; first on her husband and then on Leirwg, that it was almost impossible for her now to decide anything momentous. She had felt on familiar ground with Alaric, but Marcus was a different matter altogether. She now said: "I should like to consult my sister, Elfrida, before I give my consent to your son's wooing." So Felicius left it at that, and took his departure, after assuring Hulda that he would be everlastingly indebted to her for what she had done for his little daughter.

Chapter 29.

A Great Sorrow.

BERNARD was walking along a narrow track in the evening of the day on which Alaric had laid his father to rest. Bernard had been visiting a sick man a mile or two distant, and was now returning. His heart was lifted up in praise to God that the rule of the Druids was broken, that his converts were free to express their joy openly in songs of thanksgiving, none daring or wishing to make them afraid. He looked stronger than formerly. His life in Elfrida's home was happy and peaceful, and he was having more physical comforts than had been possible in the hut, and his health had greatly improved.

Suddenly, he paused in his walk as he noticed something out of the usual on the ground at a little distance. His eyes were not as quick to see as they had been in his youth, and he peered inquiringly a moment, then exclaimed as he saw it was the figure of a man lying face downward on the moss-covered soil. Bernard hurried on until he reached the spot. Whoever it was, friend or foe, it was some one in need. Ill perchance, dead it may be, but, no, as Bernard stooped over the prostrate figure, a face was raised to meet his gaze and Bernard cried out in surprise: "Alaric, my son, is your grief for your father so terrible as this ?

Alaric's face was swollen with tears and, even as he spoke, Bernard realised there must be some other cause of sorrow than the passing of an aged and suffering parent. Doubtless, Alaric was grieved at his loss, but his face showed signs of tremendous battle, of strain and even agony.

Bernard sat down on the ground beside Alaric and said gently: "My son, if it would help you to tell me the cause of your grief and struggle, I am a safe confidant."

As there was no response, he continued: "I wonder if it is connected with our little lady Venissa? I have long perceived that your heart was given to her."

Alaric made a great effort and pulled himself together.

"Sir, I am ashamed that you should see me in my weakness, but, oh, my heart is broken! Venissa is not for me, she is for another, and I—I am unworthy to be called a disciple of Jesus Christ, for my heart has been filled with rebellion. I have been fighting against God's will in this matter."

"Poor lad, poor lad! I can well understand how you suffer. I, too, have been where you now are. In my young days, I loved a beautiful Grecian maiden, but she was not for me. But let me tell you, Alaric, for your comfort, I have found that as I yielded to my loving Heavenly Father's will, He has been enough to fully satisfy my heart; aye, lad, He has been more to me than wife or child could have been. God is enough to fill the human heart. I notice you said, 'I have been fighting.' Do I take it that the fight is over now, my son, and that Christ is victorious?"

“Yes,” Alaric murmured. “Christ has won. I have been torn with conflict but the God of peace has triumphed. Bernard, for long I have been hearing God’s call to go up and down the land and spread the Gospel. Everywhere, doors are open, the grip of the Druids is a thing of the past. The university at Caer Isca (Exeter) is closed; now, is the day of opportunity and I, coward and selfish that I was, have been holding back, thinking fondly of home, wife and children. I have no ties, my property can be safely left in the hands of my excellent bailiff, while Osmond, I am sure, will look after my interests here, so, God helping me, I can say: ‘Here am I, send me’ ”.

Bernard rose to his feet, his eyes shining with emotion. Placing his hands on Alaric’s head, who was now in a kneeling position, the old preacher said: “Alaric, my friend, my son in the faith, go forward and the Lord go with you. Long have I also felt that God had work for you. My day is almost done, no longer can I take the journeys I could in time past, you will carry on the mission. The Lord bless you and keep you, and make His face to shine upon you, and give you His peace.”

The two were silent for a time, both feeling the solemnity of Alaric’s consecration; then Bernard, who was always practical and did not lose sight of the needs of the body, said: “Come, Alaric, come with me to Elfrida’s home; you are physically spent; you need a meal. You must remember, as you go forth on this mission, that in order to do your work for the Master, the body must not be ignored; take

reasonable care and you will be able to do more and last longer.”

So Alaric, although he would have preferred to be alone, not liking to disappoint his old friend in his kind intentions, went with him and, in the sympathetic atmosphere of Elfrida’s home, found a measure of consolation. They discussed his future work. Elfrida felt amazed that no reference was made to Venissa and, when Alaric had departed, she said to her son: “Osmond, I am bewildered at Alaric’s decision to go forth on this mission. It is beautiful to know he has heard God’s call and is willing to go, but I have for many years felt he was in love with Venissa, and what could be more suitable? Now, is it that she is willing for this sacrifice? Can you tell me what it means for her?”

"Mother mine, I thought as you do, before the coming of Marcus; since then, I have seen that Venissa's heart is not given to poor Alaric. She loves him as a brother, and Alaric realises this. Venissa's happiness is more to him than his own. Such is his love."

"Poor Alaric! I am sorry for him."

Elfrida's whole soul ached for her young friend, and she lifted up her heart in prayer that he might be comforted of God. She felt a little vexed with her niece and remarked to Osmond: "I am not sure that a marriage with a Roman is going to be the best for Venissa. Perhaps, Hulda would be wise if she refused her consent and then, after a time, Venissa might turn back to Alaric."

"I doubt, mother, if Aunt Hulda could act firmly now on any matter, she is so broken in body and spirit. Besides, we all want Venissa to be happy. Alaric wants it most of all; he would not have her coerced."

"The point is, will she be happy? Does she know her own mind, and is it wise to let her judge for herself? It has always been the custom among us that the parents should choose for the young people, but times change, and Venissa has no father. I must say I liked what I saw of Marcus when he was staying with Hulda, but then, Alaric has been as another son to me; we do not know Marcus in the same way. I must spend more time with Hulda, while Placidia is at her home and see what I think of her. A mother-in-law can often make or mar a woman's happiness. I expect Hulda will turn to me for advice."

"No doubt, she will, mother, for she has always been one to be guided by others and, you being her elder sister, what more likely than she should seek your aid in the matter now that Cynvelin is no more, and Leirwg gone."

"What has become of Leirwg I wonder?" Elfrida said.

"I have no idea," her son answered.

"I do hope he will never return to this neighbourhood," Elfrida remarked.

"I think it is very unlikely," Osmond replied.

"And all the priests scattered by the closing of the university; where have they gone?"

"To different parts of the land, or even to foreign countries, I believe, Mother. They will still be working for their religion, I fear."

"Yes, but their power is broken, at any rate, in our land. Oh, how thankful I am their grip is loosened and we are free! How wonderful it is that God brings good out of seeming evil! Years ago, our forefathers thought it a terrible thing that the Romans had conquered us, but now see what we owe to them; this deliverance from Druidism."

Next day, Elfrida went to her sister's home and spent some hours there. She was pleased to see that Placidia seemed genuinely fond of Venissa and, as the weeks passed and Placidia and her daughters were still Hulda's guests, Elfrida saw that Venissa would be welcomed in the Roman family.

Hulda told her sister of what Felicius had said, and the two felt they could only wait until Marcus came and then see if he would take that opportunity of seeking Venissa's hand. Both mother and aunt agreed to say nothing to Venissa.

Alaric was busy making his preparations for a prolonged preaching tour. Osmond was with him a great deal. He had readily consented to act as overseer for Alaric's estate.

"It will be my share of the work," Osmond said. "I do not feel the call to it myself. There is much work to do here for God, but I can attend to your affairs and so set your mind at rest to go forward."

"Do you know when Marcus is expected?" Alaric asked.

"Soon now, I think. His mother is daily looking out for him. Why do you ask?"

"I should like to have an interview with him before I start. I do not want him to hold back on my account. If he loves Venissa, as his father says he does, and if Venissa loves him, then I would rather know she was happy before I set out."

"Alaric, you are indeed noble. I fear I could never be so unselfish as you are."

"You would be, Osmond, once you truly loved. It is not real love but selfishness that seeks its own happiness rather than the happiness of the one loved."

"I really feel almost cross with Venissa, turning aside from such faithful love as yours for another whom she has known such a short time."

"No, Osmond, do not speak or feel thus. Love is a wonderful thing; it seems so beyond our control; it creeps into the heart before one is aware of its coming; it refuses to come at our own bidding, or the bidding of another. Do not censure our little Venissa. I have no blame for her. God bless her and give her happiness, I pray."

Again, Osmond said: "You are noble, Alaric. Such unselfishness passes my understanding altogether."

And Alaric, being only human, felt a ray of comfort steal into his heart at his friend's appreciation.

Chapter 30.

Her Big Brother.

THERE were moments when Venissa felt a great longing to be alone. She grew a little weary of constantly entertaining her guests, seeing that they lacked no comforts, and that the younger ones had suitable amusements. Besides which, her mother needed a good deal of consideration for, though at times Hulda made an effort to be her old self, the years of anxiety and anguish had so broken her, that the effort soon failed and she was a poor invalid, clinging to Venissa for support.

It was with a sense of relief that Venissa found herself free one day. Elfrida was spending the day with her sister, and Venissa mentioning that she wanted to visit a sick person who lived about a mile away, Elfrida suggested that Venissa should take the opportunity of going that afternoon.

"The walk will do you good, dear. Do not hurry. I can stay here until dusk. I shall enjoy a talk with your guests, and I will do anything for your mother that she needs."

Venissa thanked her aunt and decided to do as she said. She was not sorry, when the afternoon came, to find Canace, Flora and Julia happily engaged in making a house in the sand heap.

"A real, Roman villa," they told her, when she went to see what they were doing."

"Here is the *villa urbana*, here the *villa rustica*, and we are now making the *villa fructaria,*" Flora explained. "Julia only knows British houses. I want her to understand what a Roman villa is like."

As the children all seemed happy, Venissa went off after giving instructions to Amelia to keep an eye on them, and see that Flora did not do anything too unreasonable, as that young person was quite capable of doing.

She paid her visit and started on her homeward way. It was a lovely summer evening. The day had been hot; now, a little breeze had sprung up and the coolness was welcome. Venissa was in no hurry, and she lingered a while by a rippling stream over which there was a large clapper bridge. She was thinking how different were her feelings as to her safety now, from what they were on the day when she was suddenly set upon by the priests and carried off. Then, as now, she had been visiting the sick, and never to her dying day would she forget the horror when twenty men had surrounded her and, gagging her so that she was unable to cry out for help, had borne her in a half-fainting condition to the hut in the woods. She lifted up her heart in praise to God that those days of peril were over.

Long she sat lost in thought when, suddenly, she heard her name. She sprang to her feet, the colour in her face fading for a moment and then returning to bring a rosy tint to her cheeks.

"Venissa, I wondered if I should find you here. I arrived an hour ago, and your aunt told me in what direction you had gone. Venissa, have you a welcome for me?"

“Oh, Marcus, you have taken me by surprise. I came out to be alone. I felt the need of solitude,” she said with a mischievous glint in her eye.

“And I have broken rudely in on that solitude; but, tell me, are you not pleased to see me? Oh, Venissa, have you no welcome for me? I have lived for this moment, always fretting at the delay, but my father seemed in no hurry to allow me to come before. Now, at last, I am here; dear, will you give me the right to take you away with me when I have to leave? I have loved you since the day I saw you seated at Bernard’s feet at the door of the old hut. Tell me, dear one, is there any hope of my winning your love?”

Although Venissa’s reply was almost inaudible. Marcus seemed satisfied. The moments passed rapidly as happy moments have a knack of doing. They were indifferent to, and almost unconscious of the waning of the light, until Venissa suddenly exclaimed: “Marcus, I must be going home, my mother will be needing me.”

Then, at the mention of her mother, her thoughts became grave.

“Marcus, what am I thinking about? How utterly selfish I am. I am forgetting my mother. I cannot leave her in her loneliness and weakness. She needs me and I must put her first. Marcus, we must forget all we have said to each other today.”

“Venissa dearest, that is impossible. Surely we shall find a way out of the difficulty. Would not your mother make a home with us?”

“I do not think she would be persuaded to make such a complete change in her life. She is weak and showing signs of age. Somehow she seems older than Aunt Elfrida. Being a Christian seems to have renewed Aunt’s youth. And, Marcus, did you not say just now that probably after a term of years here you would be recalled to Rome? You said how you would enjoy showing me the beauties of that wonderful city.”

“My darling, I shall not give you up so easily.”

“Don’t tempt me, Marcus. My duty to my mother must come first. I am all she has, and she has suffered greatly, and is very broken now.”

Marcus was not convinced that there was no solution to the problem. His lips set in a firm manner, well-known to his soldiers. It looked as though he was not going to give up without a struggle.

However, he only said at the moment: "Dearest, we must find out what your mother thinks before we decide anything. Leave it to me."

"Don't say anything to-night, Marcus. In fact I think you had better say nothing at all."

At which remark Marcus only laughed.

There was no need to say anything in the home circle, both Hulda and Placidia guessed what had taken place.

Placidia kissed Venissa when saying good-night, and whispered: "Dear, don't disappoint Marcus. He is a good son, and will make you a good husband."

"I don't think it will ever be," Venissa said vaguely. "I cannot leave my mother."

"Oh, tut, tut! The young birds have to leave the nest," Placidia said, and would probably have added much more, but Venissa, disinclined to discuss matters with her, said courteously "Good-night, I hope you will sleep well," and disappeared.

Going to her mother's room, she found Hulda tearful. In her weakened state the presence of guests was almost too much for her. Venissa had some trouble in soothing her mother. She chafed her hands, brushed her hair and at length Hulda grew drowsy. The last words she said before falling asleep were: "My darling, what should I do without you?"

Venissa left the room meaning to seek her own apartment, when Amelia, who was waiting to attend her young mistress in her preparations for the night, said : " Master Alaric is here, Mistress Venissa, and he wants speech with you, if it is not too late."

Venissa hastened to the living-room where she found her friend awaiting her arrival. She had not seen him for several days for Alaric had been avoiding her. Now she was struck by a subtle, indescribable change in his face. Afterwards, she said to herself:

"Alaric's face reminded me of dear father's as he lay waiting for the grave, for he looked like one who had finished with the buffetings of life, and had found a peaceful haven."

Alaric smiled as Venissa entered and said: "Your big brother has come to say 'good-bye' to you, dear."

"Are you going so soon, Alaric?"

"Yes; I start at dawn tomorrow, going first to Caer Wyn and after that I know not. I am looking up for guidance. Bernard hopes I shall eventually reach the king's court, for there is a prince there, Prince Lucius, a descendant of our brave Queen Boadicea. He has been educated in Rome and Bernard has heard a rumour that he has embraced Christianity. I must go a step at a time as God shall lead. I look to my friends here to help me by prayer."

Venissa's eyes filled with tears.

"Oh, Alaric, how we shall all miss you! Indeed, we will pray for you every day; you can be sure of that."

"Dear," Alaric said, "you must not weep for me. I want you to be happy; you and Marcus deserve the best."

"Alaric, I cannot accept Marcus. How can I leave my mother? She would be desolate without me."

Alaric pondered. Then he said: "A way will be found out of the trouble, dear little sister. Don't worry. Don't turn from the love of a good man. It is God's gift to you; take it as such and be thankful. My longing is that you both may find happiness and usefulness; you and Marcus together. Now I must go. Good-night and goodbye, dear one. God bless and keep you from all evil."

Alaric stooped and, lifting Venissa's hand, kissed it, and then as tears blurred Venissa's vision he was gone. She flung herself down on the bear-skin rug which covered the couch, and hid her face in her hands. How long she would have remained there is uncertain, had not Amelia come in, and firmly insisted on her young lady going to bed.

Late as it was, Alaric felt he still had something more to accomplish, before he retired for the night. He was glad to find Elfrida, Bernard and Osmond still up. Bernard had been reading to them from his parchment rolls and expounding the Scriptures to them and, in their joy, the time had passed unheeded.

They welcomed Alaric warmly, and Osmond asked if all was ready for the early start. He intended accompanying Alaric for half a day; the two were great friends and Osmond felt the coming separation keenly.

"All my own affairs are settled happily," Alaric replied, "but there is one thing I want to put before you, dear people. You are friends of Venissa and wish her well, so I do not feel I am betraying her confidence if I tell you of her perplexity. To be brief, as it is getting late, Venissa feels she cannot accept Marcus' offer of marriage because she cannot leave her mother. I long to know Venissa's happiness is secured before I go forward. Can you suggest any solution to the problem?"

Osmond and Elfrida both spoke at the same moment.

"Why should not Hulda make her home here?"

Elfrida added: "She can bring her two personal attendants, Amelia and Hubert, with her. And when she is under Bernard's teaching, maybe she will be won for the Master."

Alaric gave a sigh of relief.

"That would be good. Do you think she will be likely to consent to the proposal?"

"I hope so," Elfrida answered. "I am sure her love for Venissa will make her willing for some sacrifice, and really I think a change of surroundings would be good for her. There in her home she broods over the loss of her husband, and the place seems haunted with memories of Leirwg and his evil influence."

"Well, then, I leave it to you to do your best to bring this to pass," Alaric said and rose to go. Bernard spoke for the first time: "Let us commend you to God once again, my dear young friend."

So together they knelt and Bernard prayed for Alaric in words of fervent supplication, long to linger in the young man's memory.

Chapter 31

Hopes For The Future.

NEXT morning, Venissa rose with a headache and a heavy heart. She reproached herself for causing Alaric sorrow; she saw no way of giving Marcus joy, and her usual bright spirit was clouded.

During the process of dressing, she recalled some words of Bernard's spoken to her long before.

"Remember," he had said, "that now you are God's child, He has His plans for your life. Nothing comes by chance. He orders all, and will guide your footsteps. A trial comes, God will work it together for your good. Trust Him."

Venissa sank on her knees by her couch and prayed for forgiveness for her unbelief which was causing her to worry; she asked for guidance, for willingness to walk in the pathway of God's planning and, as she prayed, peace came back to her heart and mind, and she was able to sing:

"Christ is my Guide in the pathway of life:
Christ is my Peace, the Dispeller of strife;
Grace He will give me His will to obey,
Led by Him gently each step of the way."

It was with a serene face Venissa was able to meet her mother and their guests at the breakfast table.

Half-way through the meal, Placidia remarked that it was time they were getting home. She turned to Hulda and said: "I can never thank you for all your kindness both in welcoming us here and in your care of my little daughter. We shall have to bring her back to see you sometimes while we are stationed in Britain or, perhaps, you could come and visit us."

Before any one else could make a remark, Flora said to Julia: "There I told you, you were coming with us, but you didn't believe me."

To every one's distress, Julia burst into tears. Marcus put his arm around her seeking to comfort the child, but she struggled from his embrace crying noisily, saying: "Don't touch me, Marcus-man. I won't go with any of you. I 'long to my 'Nissa, and I'll stay with her."

She grew so hysterical that Venissa had to carry her into another room, while Hulda said: "Poor child, she has suffered so in the past, and she has not got over the terror of it all."

"I don't know what is to be done," Placidia said with a puzzled frown on her face. "The child is not strong and she will fret herself into an illness I fear, if we take her away."

Marcus was whispering something to Canace and, in response to what he said, Canace, who always loved to please her brother said: "Please, mother, may Flora and I go?"

Placidia gave her permission, and when the children had gone, Marcus said, turning to Hulda: "Lady, may I suggest a way out of the difficulty? Will you give me Venissa? I love her and would like to make her my wife. I can assure you, she will be received into our family with joy and will be honoured and esteemed by us all, while I would lay down my life to serve her."

A look of fretfulness and uncertainty came into Hulda's face.

"I don't know what to say. I cannot decide hurriedly. You had better leave Julia with us until she is older."

"But the longer she stays, the harder the wrench will be to leave, the bond will have grown stronger," Placidia answered, while Marcus sat silent in gloom.

"Anyhow, I suppose you can wait a day or two for Hulda's decision, can you not, Marcus?" Placidia continued.

"Yes, certainly, I must. But, dear lady, do not break our hearts," he said turning to Hulda.

Hulda rose from the table as though dismissing the subject, and Marcus sought Venissa.

Julia was soothed now and Venissa had left her with Amelia, telling the woman to keep the child away from the others. With the exception of Canace, they all seemed to have an irritating effect on the poor little girl.

Marcus' face grew still gloomier, as Venissa assured him her first duty was to her mother and, unless she gave a full and free consent, she could not entertain for one moment the thought of leaving her parent.

"Do not fret, Marcus," she said gently. "Do we not profess to trust in our Heavenly Father's planning for us; we must wait His time and not snatch at happiness? When He sees fit He will place this good gift in our hands. Do you remember Bernard reading to us from the Psalms of David. 'That Thou givest them they gather'? We do not want to gather that which is not His giving."

"Ah, my Venissa, you are far above me in your spiritual experience. I am unworthy of you, and also of my Lord, but I do want, in spite of my impatience and eager desire, to please Him."

The two were making up their minds to a long time of separation, but, before the day passed, their outlook was changed.

Elfrida, according to her promise to Alaric, lost no time in seeking an interview with her sister. She was glad to be able to see her alone, for Venissa had taken her guests for a row on the river. Canace and Flora had been longing for this treat and, now that Marcus had come and the weather was good, they were able to carry out the plan.

In two coracles, each with a capable slave to manage the craft, they went off, Venissa, Marcus and Julia in one, Placidia, Canace and Flora in the second. Julia had recovered her spirits for the time being, although her eyes were still red as the result of her recent storm of tears. They all enjoyed the river scenery, and were merry together, forgetful for the moment of possible separations.

Meanwhile, Elfrida was putting her proposal before Hulda. Hulda was tearful at first, full of self-pity. Why was such a hard fate hers? Her husband gone, her religious guide had disappeared, and now her child wished to leave her.

Elfrida spoke a trifle sternly.

"Hulda, you really cannot lament that Leirwg has vanished. Think what his presence here meant. Why you would have been without a daughter, without a sister, without a nephew and many friends, if he had had his way. Consider what we owe to Marcus coming so quickly to the rescue."

"I know all that, but I am so tempest-tossed. I sometimes feel haunted. Just lately I have had periods of rest but I cannot entirely shake off the spell of the priests and the fear of the gods."

"Hulda, dear heart, I believe it is the devil, the great enemy of our souls and of our Lord Jesus Christ, who is seeking to keep you in his grip. It is he who is at the back of all the evil of our old religion; the gods are nothing, but the devil is a real foe."

Hulda looked round with wild eyes, and Elfrida began to fear for her reason, but she said firmly; "Hulda, God can deliver you. Listen, I am now going to ask Him, in the Name and for the sake of Christ, to save you from this terror and give you His spirit. Will you really put your heart into the petition with me?"

"I will, I will. I would give anything for rest. My thoughts terrify me; if I fall asleep, I awake shaking with fear."

Poor Hulda; long had she served false gods and, at the back of them, the devil. Not easily does he let his captives escape his grip.

Elfrida knelt beside her sister, holding her hand with a firm yet loving clasp, and prayed. It seemed to Elfrida that she could feel the struggle going on. It was no light thing that Hulda had so long yielded herself to please the gods and the priests, and now the fight was fierce. Hulda sobbed and groaned in mental agony, but Elfrida continued to cry for help to God Who hears His children's prayers and, gradually, Hulda's tears ceased and calm fell upon her.

Presently, Elfrida said: "Now, dear, will you not pray for yourself?" and with broken sentences Hulda asked for forgiveness, for rest and deliverance. The triumph of Calvary was made good, as together Elfrida and Hulda sought victory.

After a time, Elfrida again pressed Hulda.

"Dearest, I do feel a complete change will be good for you. Come and make your home with me. You will have Bernard to teach you more of the Good News and you will have the joy of knowing you have made Venissa and Marcus happy, to say nothing of Placidia who is longing to take her little daughter with her. It is a sacrifice for you, I know, but it is the common lot of the older ones in life to sacrifice for the younger. We have had our day, and now we must stand aside for them."

Elfrida's reasoning prevailed and Hulda said quietly: "I will come to you Elfrida. It is good of you to be willing to have a poor, broken soul as I am. It may not be long; I will spend my closing years with you."

My dear, you must not talk like that. You have many years before you yet. You are not old and, with God's blessing, you will grow stronger in mind and body, and live to be useful."

Hulda smiled faintly.

"You think your God is able to do this," she said.

"*Our* God, you mean, dear. Yes; He is able. You can see for yourself what He has done for me".

Hulda lifted her eyes heavenward. "Yes; I will say it; *our* God, *my* God. I will trust in Him."

Hulda made Venissa and Marcus very happy when they came back that evening. Placidia also was delighted, and Julia signified her willingness to go anywhere Venissa went. So it was arranged that Julia should remain in Hulda's home until the time when Marcus should return to claim his bride. He assured Venissa it would not be long delayed; he felt sure his father would give his consent for a speedy marriage. Of that Marcus had little doubt.

"It is more than I deserve," Marcus said to himself as he lay awake that night, too happy to sleep.

Chapter 32.

"Poor Leirvg!"

IT was a happy domestic scene on which the sun shone one brilliant June morning, some ten years later.

The setting of the scene was Osmond's pleasure garden. Seated there was Hulda, so changed that someone, not having seen her since the days of Venissa and Marcus' betrothal, would scarcely have known her. With peace of mind, which brought renewed health, she had grown plump and her face told its own glad tale of quiet rest of spirit.

In her arms she held a bonny baby boy of seven months, while at her feet played a little two-year-old girl. Amelia stood in the background. She had just remarked: "Lady, shall I not take baby

Alaric? Mistress Canace warned me you were not to hold him too long and get tired. He is so active that he wearies most of us."

"No, Amelia, I am not tired. Sit down yourself and rest. You get tired more quickly than I do nowadays. Ah, here comes baby's mother and father."

A sweet-faced young woman came across the green lawn, accompanied by a stalwart man. The little maiden ran to meet them, and, clinging to the man's legs, said: "Lift Ida up. Give Ida ride."

"Say 'please' darling," the mother said gently, as the father complied with his little daughter's demand.

"How well Osmond looks," Hulda remarked, as Osmond cantered around to please Ida. "You and he, Canace, are so happy in every way, it shows itself in your faces."

Canace smiled. She was just her own, charming self, the sunshine of her husband's home; the joy not only of his heart, but also of Elfrida and Hulda.

Presently, Osmond came back, declaring that he must rest after such a canter round. Ida pouted for a moment, saying. 'Do it adain, do it adain."

Canace drew her attention to some daisies growing in the grass, and suggested her picking some for Grandmother. They had not been seated together long before Hubert came from the house. He waited a moment in silence. Then Osmond said: "What is it, Hubert? You look pleased !"

"Master, I have good news. Master Alaric has arrived."

All sprang to their feet with exclamations of pleasure.

"This is splendid. He has not visited us for three years," Osmond said. "Is he well?"

"He looks tired, Master, but says he is well. He is with Mistress Elfrida, and she bade me fetch you all."

Hulda had placed the baby in Amelia's arms, and Canace told Ida to remain in the garden.

Hubert was right in saying Alaric looked tired, but his face had the expression of a happy man. There was a serenity in his countenance, and Canace said to herself: "Whatever trials Alaric has had, he is yet fully satisfied."

There were joyous greetings between the friends. Alaric wanted to see the children and made inquiries for various friends and neighbours.

"Now, we want to hear all your news," Osmond said, but Elfrida intervened.

"Alaric must have a meal and a rest; later in the day we will gather to hear his story at our leisure. Bernard will be in then; he is visiting now."

It was evening before Alaric started to talk, for, after he had eaten, Elfrida had made him lie down in a quiet room and, to his own amazement, he had fallen asleep and slept for some hours.

Now, he declared himself abundantly refreshed and glad to have a time of talking with his friends.

"I have a feeling," said Osmond, "that you have news for us somewhat out of the ordinary."

"You are right," was Alaric's reply. "Let me see; it is three years since I was here. Of the first year of my absence, I have little to tell, I was travelling towards London lingering in various places preaching the Good News."

"Were you well received?" Bernard asked.

Bernard was lying on a couch, for he was very frail now. His friends marvelled that he was still with them for, as far as they knew, he was nearly ninety and, in spite of his great age, was able to do a little visiting among the Christians.

"Evidently, my Master thinks my work is not yet done," he sometimes said.

Now, in reply to his question, Alaric said: "On the whole, yes. As in former days, so it is now, some accept the truth, some refuse; but in several places I was able to start gatherings for worship. I hope soon to visit these places again and see how the converts are getting on. At the close of that first year, I found myself welcomed at the king's court. King Lucius, whom you know is called Lever Maur, meaning 'Great Light', is a Christian. He is anxious to spread Christianity throughout his domains, and we who seek to do the work are under his protection."

"Happy days have dawned for Britain," Osmond remarked. "What a contrast to the former days when the Druids had us in their grip."

"Yes, indeed, praise God, but you know, there are special temptations connected with easy days. People are apt to get slack towards the things that matter most. The devil is still a wily foe and knows how to hinder the work of God. Well, I stayed at the court nine months, then started to work my way back here to Devon. When I reached Caer Wyn I found Marcus and Venissa had just returned from their five-year stay in Rome. They will be coming here, as soon as Marcus gets a holiday."

Hulda flushed with pleasure at the thought of a visit from her daughter, and Canace exclaimed with joy: "Oh, how lovely! I do want to see Marcus, and Venissa too."

"Are they well?" Hulda asked.

"Yes; in splendid health. They have three little ones now; the eldest, Cynvelin, you saw before they went to Rome; now, there is Felicius, and the youngest, Bernard."

"All boys?" several voices spoke at once.

"Yes; all boys, but they seem quite satisfied. Ida will be important as the only girl in the family. Her cousins will think a lot of her. Julia was with them. She has grown so like Venissa, not in looks, of course, but in her tone of voice and little mannerisms. If I closed my eyes, I could think I was speaking to the Venissa of the olden days."

Alaric paused. Although time had brought a measure of healing to his sore heart, yet even now it needed his manly self-control to speak naturally of Venissa.

"Of course, both Marcus and Venissa insisted on my making their home my headquarters while I was in that neighbourhood, which was convenient for my work."

Again Alaric paused, and more than one of his hearers thought: "Convenient, yes; but a tug at his heart strings all the time."

"I had been there about ten days," he continued, "when, visiting in a village some five or six miles distant, a woman who had received the

Gospel, having heard it from Marcus and Venissa when first they settled in Caer Wyn, said to me: 'I wonder, sir, if you could do anything to help an old, mad man who wanders in the woods here. He is always muttering some words, the same sentence over and over again; some words about darkness and light. He is in a shocking condition and most people are terrified of him. I put food for him sometimes in a hollow tree on the outskirts of the wood, and it always disappears.' "

"I said I would certainly seek to help him, if I could find him; but I wondered if I were likely to meet him. The woman thought I probably should, if I were riding through the woods. However, I saw nothing of him that day but, not long after in that neighbourhood, in a lonely spot, I heard a voice shouting: 'Men love darkness rather than light, because their deeds are evil.' I at once thought, 'can this be Leirwg?' and went in the direction of the voice and came face to face with the poor old creature--filthy, clad only in a ragged sheepskin; white hair and beard matted with mud; eyes red and nails like birds' claws. He shrieked at the sight of me and fled. I caught the words he was still shouting, as he ran: 'Men love darkness rather than light, because their deeds are evil.' I felt almost sure it was Leirwg. Leirwg, who had always been so immaculate in his person and clothing; Leirwg, who had always loved the good things of life; Leirwg, reduced to this awful condition.

My first impulse was to leave him to his fate. Why should I do anything for the man who had so persecuted others. I am ashamed to confess this, but a feeling of intense loathing overcame me for a time; then, I remembered the love of God for us poor sinners in our condition of sin and misery and, crying to God for forgiveness, I followed the old man. I soon overtook him and, when he saw I was drawing nearer to him, I saw to my horror that, reaching a dark, deep pool, he flung himself into its depths. It was not easy work rescuing him, for he struggled greatly and, in spite of his age, he was strong. At last, I managed to drag him to the bank, and even then it was difficult to climb on to firm ground. We slipped back more than once, for he was a heavy weight; at length, however, we were in safety."

"I suppose you plunged in and risked your own life in doing so?" Osmond interrupted.

"Oh, well, there was no other way of saving him, and you know I can swim. Still, we were both exhausted by the time we were out. The water had washed the old man's face, and I saw I had made no mistake. It was Leirwg."

Alaric's listeners exclaimed. "To think you really had encountered Leirwg!"

"I had to get assistance, as he was unconscious. Fortunately, I soon found two men, and we got him to the house of the woman who had first told me about him. When Marcus and Venissa heard what had taken place, they insisted on the poor old creature being brought to their villa. He did not recover complete consciousness until he had been in his new home for some days. He was constantly muttering the same sentence. 'Men love darkness rather than light, because their deeds are evil.' Then, one day, when Venissa was sitting beside him, he suddenly raised himself and screamed, 'Go away Venissa; why have you come to haunt me? I burned you in the fire. I watched the flames devour you. I have seen it ever since, and now you have come back to torment me.' "

" 'No, no,' Venissa said. 'I was never burnt. It is not a ghost you see but the real Venissa.' 'Not dead, not dead!' he gasped. 'The flames: the flames, how did you escape?' 'The flames were not kindled when I was a captive: you are thinking of the time when poor Ida was sacrificed,' Venissa told him."

"Was he sensible enough to take in the Gospel story which I am sure you all told him?" Elfrida asked.

"I cannot say," Alaric answered. "At times, he seemed to listen, and when Venissa sang to him, he grew calm. Once he said to her, 'Sing of the Christ, the One Whom you worship'. Venissa sang:

"Christ of the Father, the conquering Word,
Christ the one Leader of saints of the Lord,
Wisdom that sat on the throne of creation,
Patience unswerving through all tribulation.

Christ the Good Shepherd Who died on the tree
Redemption to purchase for you and for me;
If we but trust Him our sins to blot out,
Life everlasting we'll have without doubt."

"At first, his paroxysms of fear or of rage, I hardly know which they were, were terrible. It was as much as Marcus and I could do to hold him. Marcus had to forbid Venissa coming into the room at such times. But the care and the kindness he received made a difference to his poor, distraught mind. However, he was a physical wreck, and had evidently suffered from hunger and cold as well as from haunting memories. Altogether, he was a sad and sorry sight, making one realise what a horrible thing it is to serve the devil and what a joyous, glad thing it is to be a subject of the Heavenly King."

"Did he linger long?" Osmond queried.

"Some weeks, getting gradually weaker."

"I hope he showed gratitude to you all," Bernard remarked.

"I think he felt grateful for, one day, Venissa was attending to him and she had just washed his face and brushed his hair when he looked up earnestly at her and said: 'You, you whom I wronged, you and your poor father.' "

"Poor Leirwg! Perhaps, if the Gospel had been brought to him in his young days, he might have been different," Bernard said. "But, thank God, the grip of the Druids is a thing of the past in this land. The Gospel Light has shone. God grant that the enemy of us all may not have other snares and other perils with which to capture souls in Britain. The responsibility which rests on us is great, and it is only by His enabling power that we shall go forward, lifting the Gospel Light on high, both for ourselves and for other peoples. God grant us His grace."

And the little group of listeners said a heartfelt " Amen."

OTHER MAYFLOWER PUBLICATIONS

A Light Shines in Poland - R.K.Mazierski

John Wycliffe: The Dawn of the Reformation - David Fountain

Isaac Watts Remembered - David Fountain

Hymns and Spiritual Songs - Isaac Watts

Tony - Vivienne Wood

Lord Radstock and the Russian Awakening - David Fountain